ABOUT
THE
GIRL
WHEN THAT DAY COMES

THABANG MODIBA

©Thabang Modiba 2014

ISBN-978 0 620 57509 6

Designed by
Alexander Lubbers & Cedrick Mkhabela

To my lovely mother, Grace, my precious little sister, Monene, my mentor, Patrick & all who believed in me. May the Lord of peace give you wisdom, knowledge and understanding, for without them we perish.

With all my Love,
Thabang

1

What a lovely day, a beautiful sunny day. At least that's what I thought. Little did I know that the same day was about to turn into a disaster. I looked at the door handle in my hands and chuckled. I had forgotten all about the wrecked door. It was my father who fixed it with old rusty wires, that's the reason why it didn't take long before it fell off again. Just yesterday, mom tried opening it, and to her surprise, she had the whole door in her hands. She just got lucky it did not hurt her. My father worked at one of the country's biggest mines, made a fortune but we never saw even a single cent. He had leaking pockets and they seemed to drop everything to the ground when it was time for him to come home. He never used his money to help with anything in the house. My smile slowly faded away as I tried to find a valid reason for my father's behaviour. He brought so much pain in my heart each time I thought of him. He was like an old horse that cannot be tamed. He turned into this abusive alcoholic who cared less about anything but beer. He only came home once in two weeks and that was if we were lucky, otherwise the whole two months could pass by without him coming home, and by the time he did, there would be fights all over. Even at the shebeens, where he was supposed to be having fun with his friends, he caused troubles. It was a pity that his son was less trouble than he was. As for mom…my poor mother, she wept day and night, praying to God to keep her husband safe wherever he was. How many of the women nowadays could stand for these afflictions? I would ask myself with no answer. But thanks, she didn't jump to the roof, otherwise our house would have turned into a hell, with the devil on his feet. I remember this other day, when he came home during month end, penniless, no plastic bags for us to run for lollipops and cheese curls— raising the eyebrows of the neighbours. There was something that my father could never forget, something that make men's minds cloudy, stagger and kiss the ground. He had this small transparent bottle that fitted in the inner pocket of his jacket. If he took one or two gulps, he began to frown like a cock, shook his head and turned into a wild animal. It was as if it tempered with some of the screws inside the head. When mom greeted him, he just fumed like an old ox not ready to be spanned, and she would find herself in a boxing ring, receiving punches and insults. Silently, I would tiptoe to the corner for safety, biting my lower lip wishing I could grow big, grab his neck and throw him into the dustbin. Why all this? Guilty conscience, something whispered in my ears. Not to be questioned about his salary nor one to say, "Hello papa". He was those kinds of fathers you sometimes wish they could just disappear and never come back. At least when he was not around we had peace, with the little that mom could provide for us to survive. My mother was a strong woman, fearless and she could rip a python apart with her bare hands. With her around we were sure we could never go to bed with an empty stomach. She could smile through thick and thin, and nothing could ever get her down.

We lived in Molepo village, in an iron-correlated house which was just a shelter in disguise; it was more like staying outside. Hot as hell during summer. And if you think you could avoid the heat by staying outside under a tree, forget it. My father had cut down all the trees because he believed they were a resting place for witches at night. Icy cold during winter, even four blankets could not do one justice. Its roof had holes all over; more visible when the sun and the moon shine. When it rained, you would be welcomed by a line of tins, jars and dishes queuing for drops of water, otherwise the house would turn into a pool. Our home was just all in one. It was used as a kitchen, dining room, bathroom, and a bedroom. We would go out when our parents take a bath and vice versa. David always got angry when our mother got in while he was bathing. Sometimes mom teased him saying there was nothing David could hide from her since she was the one who used to wrap his brownish butt with nappies, and that made my brother freak out even more. My mother had a good sense of humour and we laughed a lot when we were with her, but that lasted until this very day, this day when David pushed the door so hard that it nearly fell on me, but I was lucky that it fell just next to me by the corner of the shack, nearly removing zinc that was tired and worn out, rust fell down as the door hit it. Had David forgotten all about the door? He was the last person who closed it. I remember how careful he was with it. I wondered why he did that. For crying out loud, this is my beautiful sunny day—I woke up with a huge smile on this day hoping all would go well, and now my brother ruined the door and he was standing there like a statue. It was as if he had seen a ghost. He stood there for minutes without moving or even talking and that really gave me a fright. I took David by hand and helped him sit on the chair. But I must admit, it was not an easy task to do. It was more like dragging a huge snow man. I gave him a cup of cold water and watched him tremble with it in his hand. It took him a few minutes to bring it to the lips, which were shaking like jelly. I calmly asked, 'Buti (brother), what is it? What's going on?' To my surprise, I was talking alone. David did not say anything; all he did was shiver uncontrollably. To tell the truth, he was scaring the crap out of me but I tried to act boldly. After a few minutes of what seemed like forever, he was able to utter a few words …words that made me join his shivering crew.

'Mother…mother…' he stammered.

'Mother? What about mother? What happened to mom, buti, what?' I screamed and shook David violently. I was afraid of what he was about to say, but I had to know, especially if it concerned my mother, I had to know! The last thing David said changed my life forever. It's amazing how the world works, one minute you are happy, the next you are the most miserable person anyone could ever find on the planet. 'Mom died, Dikeledi, mom…'

'Don't worry, it's just a shock. She'll be fine.'
'I hope so, sister. I can't afford losing her too.'
'It's okay, she'll be fine. You won't lose her.'
'If you say so. When will she be discharged?'
'Tomorrow morning. Will you come and fetch her?'
'No, I can't. I'll be busy helping dad with funeral preparations. I'll send someone.' Two people were talking but I could only recognize one voice, my brother's. I tried opening my eyes which were too heavy, not having to speak of the head, oh boy, it was killing me. I slowly opened my eyes and there I was, in a hospital. What on earth am I doing here? I wondered. I looked around and saw a nurse patting David's shoulder. Then David nodded and started walking towards me. 'Hey you… you are awake. How do you feel, little sis?' David grinned. I knew my brother very well, he was not okay.

'What happened, why am I…?' I didn't finish my question because I just remembered what caused this confusion. Yes, I remembered very well. An amnesia that clouded my mind for minutes left and reminded me how miserable I was. My lovely mother died, streams of tears started running down my cheeks like a waterfall. My dear mom died and the whole world shattered all over me. Suddenly, life became useless and meaningless. I wished I could have died too. For the first time in my life, I wondered what my reason for living was. My mother was my whole life, my world revolved around her.

'It's okay, little sis. You have collapsed, but Sister Florence said you'll be discharged by tomorrow.' David tried comforting me. I could see it was also hard for him. He was trying too hard to hold back the tears that filled his eyes. Before he broke down in front of his little sister, he quickly said goodbye and left. David was one of those people who believed that real men are like sheep, they never cry. So crying in front of a woman would be so embarrassing for David, it would mean he had lost his manhood. Quite frankly, the belief was just pure crap to me. It was a self-torture, a reason for many men dying of heart attacks in our village; they never shared their troubles with anyone. They believed in the so called "sheep toughness" which was slowly leading them to their early graves.

The following morning a strange man walked into our ward. He stopped in the middle of the room and started looking around as if he has lost something precious. When he faced our side, he lightened up and said, 'There she is, looking fine as ever.' Then he turned to Sister Florence, who was busy treating a patient just next to me. 'Sister, is she ready yet?' I wondered why a total stranger was concerned about my readiness. He was a strange man with strange looks. I wouldn't leave with a psychotic man whose hair was fully grown and longing for just a touch of a comb. His beard was so long, tangled like grass and dirty, with red and green fluff all over—a coloured mop. I wondered if he cared just to peep in a mirror for at least the last five days. Oh, I nearly forgot about the leather jacket he was wearing, it was describing the number of years it has been "breathing", and so were his brown leather shoes. Besides being a stranger, the man was just too messy to mess with me. He stood there looking at me with a nervous grin and I just stared right back at him without flinching. I wished he would just vanish or at least the ground could just do me a huge favour and swallowed me. I was not ready for clowns, not in my lifetime. If it's the hospital's way of cheering up its patients, then it has totally lost it. 'Hey...' The clown paused and cleared his throat. He was a little bit nervous but that did not stop him from bugging me. 'How are you, girly? Just look at you...you are so big.' I kept on staring and did not say a damn word. I was very much bored and angry since I was mourning. I was not ready for any "chit chat" especially with him. 'You must be wondering who I am...I am your uncle....' He paused as he saw me raising my eyebrows. If you are my uncle, how come I don't know you? That was all what the expression was saying. He tried removing the frustration that was written all over my face.

'Uncle Nick, remember Uncle Nick...?' Uncle Nick, I thought. Where has he been all the time? And why is he such a mess? He looked much wrecked and older than my father who was also as much of a mess as he was. Thanks, my memory came to life. He was my father's long lost friend. He used to visit our home back in the days when I was still a kid. Mom used to be very angry when he visited us because she believed Uncle Nick turned my father into a drunkard. They would leave at night for the shebeens and came back the following morning very drunk. I did not understand then, but now I do. By that time my mother was judged as an annoying old woman who did not want my wonderful uncle to visit us. I loved Uncle Nick too much because he never came empty-handed. He always brought me lollipops and chocolates, but now I hated him more than I loved him then. I understand mom better now. This was the same man who took our peace and introduced alcohol into our home. If he didn't take my father to those nasty shebeens, he would have been a loving husband and responsible father. Now my father is just a walking brewery, useless family man and a nightmare.

'How old are you now, my girl?' Uncle Nick interrupted my troubled mind, which was now provoking me to hate and hate him abundantly.

'Sixteen!' I said arrogantly. It was sure like, 'Leave me the hell alone, you home wrecker!'

'Wow! You have grown to such a big woman, huh? In what grade are you now?'

'Dikeledi, get ready. It's time to go now. You must be relieved.' Sister Florence interrupted our lousy conversation and I could not thank her enough. One more word from this man would cause me to collapse again.

'I am more than ready, sister. I just want to go home.' I sighed with relief. She gave Uncle Nick some file and pointed out for him to sign. What for? I did not know and cared less. All I wanted was to walk away from that place with a strange smell. It reminded me of so much pain, so much suffering, and never assured me of survival.

Uncle Nick quietly drove all the way home and I thanked God he got the point. I was not ready for any conversation, especially when mom was in a cold refrigerator at some silly mortuary that rejoiced at her death. It is weird how the world behaves, when others are mourning for the loss of their loved ones, others rejoice at their tears because the very tears bring food to their table. The more tears, the more the benefits.

2

I thought the day on which my mother died was the worst, not aware that the worst was yet to come. It just happened that I wake up earlier, something I rarely do. I only woke up early during school days, and that was not an easy task to do. I just dragged myself out of bed. I'm definitely not a morning person, whoever or whatever woke me up this early today, surely wanted me to see a sinful act that was taking place outside. I yawned, stretched myself and opened the door. I saw ghostly figures busy offloading what looked like wardrobe doors from a van. Oh, it is Uncle Nick and my father, I thought. I wondered where they got those remnants and what were they planning to use them for? It's my mother's funeral day, maybe they want to use that to make fire, that's what I thought, until I saw what they did next. I watched them from the beginning to the end. At first I thought it was a joke but it just turned out to be real. I watched Uncle Nick and dad put the doors together, using screws and hammers. I totally observed until the wardrobe doors became something like a coffin and that was going to bury my mother. The impossible just became possible and I am the witness. I remember one day my mother told me a story of how people in the olden days used to bury their loved ones. Apparently people then didn't have coffins, so they used animal skins to bury people. So there came an era when animal skin was out of fashion, people started creating coffins with cupboards and old doors. I was skeptical but my father was there to confirm what my mother told me. Only did I not know that the scenario would one day come to life. The scene became a nightmare, more like a horror movie. It seemed unreal, and the picture kept flashing in my mind, haunting me like hell. All these activities instilled much anger and hatred in me. I believe that even those people who were mourning at the funeral were not only mourning for the passing away of their beloved friend but also for the fact that her children were about to embark on a journey of an outrageous poverty. I was crying no more; I ran out of tears. For the first time in my life, I hated my father sincerely. How could a man who loved his wife bury her like a dog while he reported at work every single day? Each time I looked at my father, a bad feeling over-shadowed my heart. The feeling was indescribable. It was more than hatred. I just kept wondering how a normal family man could do such an evil thing without shame. He just turned us into a ridicule of the village gossipers. I saw how everyone looked at me at school. I could read their mothers' gossips written all over their faces. My best friend started avoiding me, and for what? I did not know. How could people judge one by the way her mother's funeral was? The world is such a wicked place to live in. It judges people for silly things. Poverty will judge how much love you get, money decides whether you have friends or not. I could see it with the Legodis, the village tycoons; who owned big shops and their children were treated like royalty. Everyone wanted to befriend them and how I envied them, wishing I could be part of their family. They were always surrounded by multitudes, just like flies on a rotten meat, and I believe they give a piece of cake to however smile with them. Kids at school worshiped the ground they walked on. It was a pity for us with worn out faces and nothing to carry in our pockets—no one cared whether we live or die. It was more like we didn't exist. I blamed my father for all that; it was his entire fault. How foolish can a man be? Where does he get the guards to feed kids that were not his and left his own flesh and blood to starve to death? All this information I heard from a fight my parents had one day. I realized that dad had a concubine that he was taking care of and that had grieved my mother after finding out. I didn't know how she found out, but she did. She never believed in rumours, her slogan was, "Believe it, when you see it." She hated rumours with all of her heart, and the slogan was meant for gossipers.

'Dikeledi, this is Aunt Ruth. She'll be your mother from now on…' Before dad could finish whatever he was going to say, I was already on him. I screamed like a crazy person. Please don't blame me, I was shocked and frustrated. The news hit me like a lightning and that caused me to yell at my father like one who had lost it. 'What? No. No, dad. Nobody will ever replace my mother, nobody!' It did not even take a week since my mother's burial, yet my father had the courage to bring his concubine home. You should have seen the damn woman—too out of place to replace my dear mother. She wore heavy make-up, thick red lipstick and drew double black lines under the eyelashes with an eyebrow pencil. Too many accessories for one woman—it's like a Christmas tree. She was just dramatic to be compared with my lovely mother. My mom was a respectable woman, she would never wear such tight short pants, it's so embarrassing for an old overweight woman with love handles and so much stretch marks. Okay, maybe that did not come out well, but no one on this earth could ever be compared to my beloved mother.

'What did you just say? Did I just hear you disrespect me, Dikeledi, huh?' my father asked fuming with anger. He hastily walked towards me and I, on the other hand was too damn pissed to notice that danger was coming my way. I dared talk back. 'Yes, dad, you heard me. I'm not accepting anyone for a mother, not even her!' I said, pointing at the woman who now looked like she just swallowed a lemon juice, with her nose held high. I did not know what hit me next, but whatever it was, it hit me so hard that I staggered all the way to the other side of the table. I hit a chair and fell to the ground. I lay there for minutes without moving, by the time I decided to open my eye, I couldn't. Then my father harshly said, 'If you dare disrespect me or your aunt again, I'm afraid you'll find yourself were your mother is. I swear by my life, Dikeledi, I will kill you with these bare hands of mine!' Then he turned to his lover and calmly said, 'Let's go, honey. I'm so sorry, love.' Did I just hear my father say honey? The man who called his wife by name 'till death? There was no single day I could ever hear my father calling mom with all those sweet names that lovers usually call their loved ones, but on this very day I dare hear him call a stranger, "honey". I hated him more and more every day. I even started believing that he had killed my mother. Oh, yes! I blamed my father for my mother's death. I was sure if it was not because of him, mom would not have crossed that robot while closed. She would have noticed that it was red, but she did not because she left stressed that morning. She had a huge fight with my father the night before her death. She was not fine when she left for work that morning. She pretended to be fine for our sake, but I could see that. I remember her face very well that morning, sadness was written all over it yet she tried so hard to smile. She did that for my sake, for Naledi's sake. 'Mommy, please bring me sweets from work, lots of sweets, mommy.'

'Okay, my angel. Mommy will bring you sweets, but now I have to run to work otherwise I'll be late,' mom said to my little sister, Naledi, who was busy shaking mom's hand to get attention. My little sister was so naive, she was not aware that she was hurting mom when she swung that hand. I saw mom screwing her face with pain, as Naledi

14

kept on swinging the hand from one side to the other. I had to intervene. I pulled her away with an excuse of wanting to clothe her. I knew mom would not do anything because she loved her too much to rebuke her. Her hand had bruises due to the fight. My father was not ashamed of beating my mother right in front of me, luckily when that happens Naledi would be fast asleep otherwise that would have traumatized her. I was the only one who usually witnessed the beatings, since David was never home. Ever since my brother graduated from high school, about four years ago, he never slept home. One day mom confronted him and that did not turn out well. My poor mother was just trying to show her son that sleeping away from home was not a good thing.

'C'mon, Mom, do you really expect me to sleep with you and dad in the same room? You know I am a man now!' said my arrogant brother. 'If you seriously want me to sleep at home, you should build more rooms.' That left mom speechless. She knew David was right in some way; there was no privacy and something had to be done. David wouldn't sleep with Naledi and me on the floor; he was no longer a kid. It became a routine that everyone got used to; we knew he would come back during the day and leave in the evening. No one knew where he slept and no one dared to ask. My mother did not like it but she had to accept it, since she could not afford to build more rooms. There was a half-built shack next to the one we stayed in and it had been standing like that even before I was born. My mother tried talking to my father about building a proper house, but the poor woman would just risk being beaten up. My father would not dare beat my mother when David was around, maybe he was scared of him. There was this other time when David and dad had a quarrel, and David nearly beat dad, but my mother had stopped him. How I wish my brother could screw his neck a bit maybe it would bring sense in him. Since that day Dad and David stopped talking to each other, I bet they hated each other. They were like a rat and a mouse; when one got in, the other walked out. There was no way we could ever sit together as a family. David disliked my father so much that could make a witch to tremble, he even wished him to die. He blamed dad for not allowing him to further his studies. My brother graduated from high school with good marks, but he could not go to varsity because his father refused to pay his university fees. That really made my brother mad, he had always liked school. He wanted to be a civil engineer but all those dreams were shattered. Now my brother was just a useless gang member with no future.

'Dike, you'll take your sister to school today, I have to run to work now. I'm late,' my mother said, grabbing her handbag and then she kissed my little sister goodbye. My mother usually dropped my little sister at school before she goes to work, but on that day she would not because she woke up late. It was the result of a fight. She had bruises all over, and I could see she was feeling pain but trying too hard not to show. 'Okay, Mama,' I said, not aware it was the last time seeing her. I felt sorry for her. She was trying too hard to bring food to the table. I heard she was earning "peanuts" yet we survived with the little she made. Though she worked as a maid, she never complained. She was a hardworking woman, very bold and believed she could do anything. She even promised that she would try by all means to help me pursue my studies at university. She saved enough money for me and unfortunately the money was used for the funeral. I realized that when David argued with my father about it after the funeral. 'How could you withdraw that money, dad?' David fumed with anger. 'That money was for Dikeledi's university fees, man!' And my ignorant and less caring father said, 'So which money was supposed to buy food for the funeral, boy? Which one is more important? Food for the funeral or a stupid university fee?'

'Man...' David choked with anger. 'Man, I'll kill you. I won't allow you to ruin my little sister's future like you ruined mine. I'll kill you, man!' David said, holding my father by the collar of his shirt. Fortunately, Uncle Nick stopped him. I do not know what could have happened, but I smelt a rat.

Someone opened the door a few minutes after my father had left. I was too scared to lift my head. I thought it was him, coming back to finish me off. 'Dike,' it was David's voice. I don't know where he had been for the past three days, he had just disappeared. His tendency of leaving for days without letting anyone know really freaked me out. My brother liked bad company and mom always fought with him about that. He associated himself with corrupt boys of the village; those that everybody feared were the type of company David goes for. He was a trouble maker, like mom used to say. My brother was very arrogant; he never listened to anyone's advice, not even mom's. He was part of gang and he took pride in it. They wore a black T-shirt with large white prints, "HUSTLE BOYS" on the front, "WE DO WHAT WE HAVE TO DO" on the back. One day mom found the shirt while doing laundry. 'Where did you get this, sonny?' she asked. My brother ignorantly shrugged his shoulders and said, 'We do what we have to do to survive, mom.' Then he left, just like that.

'David….' I said, lifting my head.

'What happened to you?' David was surprised by my eye, it was swollen.

'D-dad brought some woman home. He's replacing mom, buti…' I sobbed.

'What, what?' David started going around the shack as if he had lost his mind. 'So now the dude has the nerve to bring some trash home!' David's eyes became bloodshot in a second, which usually happened when he was furious. 'And this?' he pointed at my eye.

'He hit me, dad hit me, David.' David was now dragging everything in the shack aside: chairs, plates, and clothes were flying in the air, as if they have grown wings. Finally, he got what he was looking for. He pulled a big black dagga out of his suitcase, a big scary one, and I just knew that he was up to no good. Then he stormed out of the house. David was going to the shebeen and if he found dad there, he would tear him into pieces. I ran after him. I wanted to stop him. 'Buti, buti,' I gasped. 'Where are you going? Please, stop, please…'

'Dikeledi, go back. Go back to the house, now!' I knew I had to respond to the order. Nobody wanted to mess with David when he was like that. I went back into the house and started praying, hoping he won't do anything stupid.

3

It was on a blue Monday morning when I entered the classroom, and everyone just burst into laughter. I wondered what the joke was, and why it seemed like it waited for my arrival. 'How about I told you so!' screamed a stupid boy, in the back corner of the classroom, and everybody confirmed what he was saying by whistling and giggling. I asked the girl who sat next to me what the joke was, and I found out that the "Hi Hi Ha Ha" was all me. They bet that I would come wearing my green jersey and finally they won. I didn't have a school jersey, the green one was the only one I had. I wore it at home, school, actually I wore it anytime, and everywhere, as long as it was cold. Mom had promised to buy me a jersey during month end, unfortunately she never came to see the end of it. I told myself I was not going to let a silly joke get to me, but the next one just tore me off. I don't even understand how a normal person could say what that boy said. 'And I heard...' the same silly boy continued with his silly jokes, he could not finish the sentence as he continued laughing. Everybody waited impatiently for him to finish laughing. After a few seconds of what seemed like a decade to my classmates, the same silly boy said, 'I heard her mom was buried in a tomato cardboard box, ha ha...' Then there was total silence. No one moved and no one laughed. I guess the joke everyone had been waiting for turned out to be a torture. Everybody's face was now bowed while the stupid boy was fidgeting like a wizard caught in action. I bet he wished the ground could just open and swallowed him. I guess it just slipped out, that was surely the works of his mother's gossips. Suddenly, I sprang out of the classroom to the girls' toilets. Nothing could describe how I felt, absolutely nothing.

'Yes, chomy (my friend), that's him. And you know what? All those gangsters were arrested.'

'Huh, my friend what happened?'

'It's said they robbed the Legodis' supermarkets last night'

'You must be joking, chomy. Do you mean all the "hustle boys" were arrested?'

'Yes my friend, even little Miss Green Jersey's brother was there.'

'Huh? You mean Dikeledi's brother, chomy? The charming, Davy?'

'Ye...' The girl got frozen when she got out of one of the toilets and finding me there. She didn't know whether to talk or leave and it was the same with her buddy. They just giggled embarrasedly and quickly left the place. I couldn't care less about what they said about me, but more about my family. Just a few seconds ago a foolish boy was on about my mother's funeral and now some lunatics were busy about my brother's arrest, which I was not aware of. But was it really true that my only brother was arrested? My only left hope? That was enough to take in one day. I felt like my heart was pumping right outside, on the skin exposed to harsh weathers. The pain I felt was too much for one person to bear. I let my heavy body to rest, right on the toilet floor and hygiene was the last thing on my mind. What did I ever do to deserve this punishment? I wondered. Puzzled faces passed me, going in and out of the toilets—I could sense some were there because they were told to come "check me out". The last time I saw my brother was when he left with a dagga in his hand, and then he was never back. It was at the mercy of a group of men who stopped him otherwise he would have stabbed dad to death.

Weeks passed by, day and night I remembered my brother who was in jail. Life was no longer fun for me. I was overburdened. It was as if I've been living forever, seen it all, and I was more than ready to go join mom wherever she was—dying was my choice. Really, I felt abandoned by those I love. First it was dad, then mom and now David, I bet Naledi was on her way too.
'Sis Dike, my mom is calling you,' a sweet little voice interrupted my busy thoughts. 'I've been knocking for so long and you did not answer. So I decided to come in since the door was half opened.' It was Regina Mokoena, the kid from next door, where we used to fetch water

while mom was still alive. We didn't have our own tap so we used theirs. We normally paid two hundred rand at the end of each month. Since mom died, I got ashamed of going there because no one would pay the bill. It was better before David got arrested. He usually brought us enough water when he had decided to come home and it lasted until he was back again. I don't know where he got the water from, but I was just grateful that he brought it. After David's arrest the water got finished and I had no choice but to go next door, and today I bet they wanted me to pay for that bucket of water I've asked for. I slowly stood up from the cold cement floor and followed Regina to her home. We found her mother in the kitchen, busy cooking. She was frying meat and it smelled so good, especially for us who last ate meat on the day of the funeral. Dad, David and Uncle Nick had slaughtered a goat, which was cooked on the day of mom's funeral. As from that day Naledi and I had been eating porridge mixed with water, and the maize meal was a leftover of the funeral day. At least we ate fish when David was back. He used to bring lots of tinned fish and they lasted for days.

'Dikeledi, you are here already. How are you, my girl?' Mama Regina asked, busy pouring spices on the meat. 'I just wonder where you fetch water from these days. I thought you'll be back. How is your eye?' she said, turning my head aside. I lied that day; I couldn't tell her the truth. I could not tell her that it was my father who did that to me. I told her that I hit the school gate.

'I could see it's getting better. I hope you are still using that ointment I gave you.' I just broke down in front of her. I couldn't help it; the embracing was more or less the same as my mother's. A woman's qualities of love, tender and pity— I could feel them. I knew if I got hurt or sick my mother would be bugging me with all those motherly questions: "Did you drink your medicine? Have you eaten anything? Have you had enough sleep?" I missed the love, warmth, comfort and protection I got from my mother, a lot. 'Hey kid, what's wrong? Is everything alright, dear?' Mama Regina asked, busy brushing my back. I was sobbing uncontrollably. 'Regina, please go get Dikeledi a tissue. Hurry!' she said to her daughter and then turned to me, speaking in a soft tone, a very comforting one. 'You know, my girl, you don't have to bother that much, you are still having a long way to go. God is all by your side and he won't let you suffer.' That was too big for my little head but surprisingly soothing. The woman I was with believed in God. She used to go to the same church with my mother. Sunday would never pass by; you would see her trotting to church with her child. I wiped my tears with a tissue and wished I could stay with the Mokoena family.

'Did you eat anything? Regina, give me a plate and let me dish out for her.' Regina was so energetic when she has been sent for, much more like me when I was sent by my mother. 'There you go. Eat and stop crying, it's not good for your health,' Mama Regina said, giving me food. I just stared at the plate without touching it. How could I continue eating and filling my stomach while my younger sister was out there waiting to eat porridge with water, and I would be smelling meat? That wouldn't sound good. 'Why are you not eating? Aren't you hungry, Dikeledi?' Mama Regina said, pushing the plate a bit closer to me. 'You have to eat, come on now.' I coughed to clear my throat because what I was about to say was a little bit embarrassing, but I had to say it anyway. That was what every parent would have done. 'May I…may I take the food along with me? I…'

'It's fine, eat those, and I'll make some for your sister.' It was as if she was reading my thoughts, I don't know how she did that but she was good. Phew! I sighed with relief. I ate everything in the plate, and I didn't leave a crumb for a dog. After eating, she gave me a fully filled lunchbox to take home with. 'And come fetch water, okay?' she said, opening the door for me.

'Thank you for the food but as for water, I won't have money to pay…'

'It's all right, you don't have to pay. Your mom was a very loyal friend of mine. She paid her bills very well and sometimes even in advance, so I'm doing this to honour her,' she said with a warm smile. People like her can make you believe God exist because they put a word into practice. 'Thank you, Mama. May God bless you.' That was the least I could say, the woman was just an angel from above. She made me feel alive again. I left her house feeling revived, moreover, relieved about the water issue. I was getting tired of carrying a bottle with me to school because people were even starting to suspect me.

It was on a Saturday morning when I hear a car horn outside and I wondered who it was since David was not around. He was the only one who used to annoy us with horns of his friends' cars and no one knew them. I slowly pushed away the blankets which smelled like a lavatory due to my little sister's urine. Since mom died nobody washed them. I used to help her wash them during weekends when she was not working. I dragged myself to the door to see who was bugging us with a horn so early in the morning. I rubbed my eyes and saw a white van parked next to the gate. It looked like the same van Uncle Nick drove that day he picked me up from the hospital. I came closer to it, and yes, I was right. It was the same van that was used to carry my mother to the cemetery, horrible memories indeed. Uncle Nick gave me that huge grin, the same one he used to give me when he came home back in the days. I used to run to him while he was still at the gate; I was the only one who used to see him from afar. On my way to the gate I'll scream, "Uncle," and then he'll shout, "Guess what I have for you?" and I'll childishly whoop, "Chocolates!" and he'll say, "Yep, you got me!" Then I'll grab the chocolates which were hidden in his back pockets with excitement. Uncle Nick opened the window of his van and said, 'Hello, Dikeledi. You seem to be growing bigger every day. Just look at you today.' His daily compliments about my growth were starting to annoy me.

'Hello, Uncle Nick. Dad is not here!' I said annoyingly. 'I'm not here for your dad, but for you,' he said, and I frowned. He is here for me, what does that supposed to mean? 'I hope you know what happened to David. He called and asked me to bring you to him. Your brother really needs to see you.' Uncle Nick removed the confusion that was written on my face. 'Guess you can quickly bath yourself so that we can get going.' I didn't utter any word. I quickly ran into the house and wiped my face, changed the urine smelling clothes and woke Naledi up. I couldn't leave her alone in the house. I had to take her to Regina's house. I humbly asked them to keep an eye on her until I come back. What a wonderful woman Mama Regina was, a free spirit indeed, unlike many women I knew, she never complained. I jumped into the van and off we went. On the way Uncle Nick resumed a conversation but I couldn't hear anything as my mind was occupied. I was nervous, wondering what my brother could have experienced. I heard that prison turned good people to monsters because of evil activities taking place there. Thinking of my brother who was troublesome before he went there, I just couldn't bear to think about it. 'We are finally here!' Uncle Nick said, and that's the only thing I picked up from him since we left home. I then jumped off the van and followed him through the dark shades of hell; what could be the so called jail. I never imagined myself going there, but there I was. Uncle Nick approached a man wearing a cop's uniform and talked to him while I waited on the bench. A few minutes later I was called to a small cold room and waited there impatiently. At long last my beloved brother showed up, with some cop holding him by his neck. He violently pushed David into the room and banged the door. He stood there for a while without moving, bowed down like a hobo in winter. He was chained like a real criminal. It was as if I was watching an American action movie. His feet and hands were chained, and there were bruises on his face. One of his eyes was half closed; it was as if he was stung by a queen bee. He was much thinner and so dirty, as if he was homeless. 'David, my brother.' I ran towards him with tears in my eyes, and I threw myself on him. He pushed me a bit away and I realized I was hurting him. So the bruises were not only on his face but all over his body. 'Sorry…' I said, removing my hands. We sat down and looked into each other's eyes without saying a word. After a while I decided to break the silence. 'How have you been, buti?' I asked.

'How is everything with you, little sis? How is Naledi doing? Has dad been treating you well?' David said, avoiding my question.

'Buti, why did you do this to yourself, to us, why, buti? How could you sell your life so cheap, my brother? How….' I broke down in tears. I shouldn't have said that but I did anyway. I guess that's what bugged me all the time. 'It's okay, my little sister, don't cry. I'm glad that you will not end up like me.' David softly rubbed his hands against mine. 'You are a strong young woman, Dikeledi, and I respect you for that. You remind me so much of mother. Please, promise me you won't end up like me,' David said, with tears running down his cheeks. It was the first time seeing my brother cry, I always thought of him to be this tough guy who never gets hurt. No matter what you can do to him, he'll never cry but on this day he seemed vulnerable. My tough brother shared tears with me; it seemed like a day dream in prison.

'Dikeledi, you have to promise me you will make something out of yourself. You must not end up useless like me. That's not what mom would have wished for me or you. You know I always wanted to be an engineer. I really wanted a good life. I wanted to go to university so bad but that dream was shattered. Look at me today, I'm just a useless prisoner and my life is over,' David sighed deeply. 'I can't blame our parents for not having money to take me to school but I blame myself for choosing this life, and now I'm reaping the fruits of my labour.' David's words speared through my heart. I've never heard my brother talk like that before. 'Life is a choice, my little sister. Nobody is responsible for anyone's life, not even our parents. You decide who you want to be, then you become what you choose. If you choose to be poor for the rest of your life, nature will respect your choice and then you remain as you are, but if you choose to turn your life around, so shall it be!' My brother talked so maturely and I couldn't believe it. If it was life in jail that gave him sense, then it worked.

'We owe it to ourselves to make something out of us and it affects us the most if we don't, not dad nor mom. Now you have to go back home and be a good sister to Naledi. She's only three and she's going to need a proper care. You are the only mother she's got now,' David paused a little bit and then he said, 'Promise me you'll study hard and pass your matric well. You must succeed, little sis, you must go to university and become a Chartered Accountant you always dreamed to be.'

'How will I do that when you are not around, buti? Where

will I get the resources, the support and the money to take me to university? You know dad will not agree.'

'Leave dad out of this! I told you that life is a choice; you do it for you not for dad. I know you will make it, just hang in there and do what you have to do. But never do anything illegal to achieve your goal or else you will end up like me. You are the one who always told me to have faith in myself and in God. Do you remember what you told me on that Sunday when you went to church with mom? You said faith is believing what you don't see with your natural eye, believing and hoping in the unseen before they manifest in the physical. So now you have to go practice what you preached to me.' Those last words from David touched me like nothing before, I couldn't stop crying nor believe it was my brother who said that, really jail showed me another side of my brother, a more grown up and matured creature. The door was flung open and the same cop who held my brother by his neck a few minutes ago appeared and harshly said, 'David Mafifi, your time is up. Come with me!' He dragged David to his feet and I saw my brother shrink back. 'Goodbye, my little sis. Take care of yourself and please think of what I said,' David said, as the ugly cop dragged him to the pit of hell. I thought I was done crying but my eyes said I was not. I cried until my eyes were swollen and red as blood. Uncle Nick appeared at the door, held my hand and we quickly left.

4

'How is your useless brother doing? I hope he rots in jail!'
Those were my father's spiteful words, after Uncle Nick
had dropped me at home. We found my father back after
leaving for a whole week with his concubine.

'He's fine, papa…Papa, can I get a white school shirt and
a skirt, and papa, Naledi's socks are worn out, and she'll
also need new…' Before I could finish dad was all over
the place. He was shouting like someone who had lost
one of his teeth in a battle, more like acid was poured on
him while he was still relaxing. 'What? Do I look like an
ATM machine to you? When you see me, you see money.
I'm getting tired of you kids. I only get money once in a
month and you are acting like I own a bank!'

'But papa, the principal said he'll kick me out of school if
I don't buy a uniform soon, I…'

'So what? What must I do? Cut myself into pieces, huh?
You have to start being responsible, girl! You are a big
woman now. Go get a job or rather use your femininity to

get money, man!' The words really shocked me. My own father just said I should use my femininity to get money. What kind of a father would say that to a child he loved and cared for? I knew of fathers who would die protecting their own kids, fathers who would kill to give their children a proper education, but mine did not care whether I got expelled from school or not. My father's stinginess and selfish ambitions really got in our way. I started to believe David when he said Dad was bewitched, no normal father would be so cruel to his own kids. But mom disagreed with David about that statement, she would say, 'My son, no one has bewitched your father except himself,' then my mother sighed deeply, placing her hand on my brother's shoulder. 'David, you are my only son and I want you to listen to me attentively. If it happens that you have your own family, I want you to be a better husband and a good father to your children. Do you hear me, sonny?' David nodded.

I decided to go to church the next day; I thought maybe if I prayed for dad he might change. Since mom died, I never went to church. Mom was a Christian; she loved God and never missed church. I bet she was now in heaven with the angels because she was one on earth. I bathed Naledi, then myself, took the bible and went to church. We got there a bit early and chose front seats. I really wanted to see and hear the preacher well. People at church were so friendly, they greeted everyone with warm smiles and that made me feel at home. After a few minutes, the church began. We sang songs of praise and chanted with joy as we sang choruses. Naledi was so overjoyed. For the first time after mom's death, I saw her smile. She clapped her tiny hands while jumping around the church. A tall dark skinned man came to the pulpit, carrying a huge bible, wrapped in a beautiful flowery cover. He was wearing a white suit, pink shirt, a matching pink tie and sharp nosed leather shoes. He looked neat and presentable. He greeted us with a big smile and introduced himself as Pastor Molima. He prayed for the whole congregation and then he began preaching the gospel. The title of his message was "DO NOT WORRY". It was as if he was talking to me, as if someone told him what I was going through. He asked us if by worrying we added a day to our lives, and he gave us a principle to use every day of our lives when we encounter worry.

'If you start worrying ask yourself whether you are adding a day to your life or subtracting it. If you have added, then continue worrying, if you have subtracted, stop worrying and rather look for a solution,' Pastor Molima said. That's when I realized that worrying has never added a day to my life, but it brought stress, headaches, pains and all those sort of bad things that could even lead to one's early death. I wished the message was preached on one of the Sundays while my mother was still alive. Maybe she would have used the principle of worry and maybe she would still be alive. I felt lighter after church. It was as if a heavy load was removed from my shoulders. I used to ask my mother why she liked church so much, and she'll tell me she went there to offload heavy loads, and when she comes back, she'll be fresh and young again. Then she'll say, 'I also go there to take strength for the week ahead, and when the strength gets finished by Saturday, I go for another on Sunday, that's why I never run out of strength. You see, baby, that's why you should never miss a single Sunday without going to church, otherwise you won't have enough strength for the week ahead .' I would smile wryly because I thought what she was saying was silly, but now I know the truth. On this very Sunday, I felt what mom always talked about. I felt strengthened and ready to face the week ahead.

'I guess you know why I called you in my office,' said our school principal, Mr Morema, the tallest giant I've ever seen. A scary man who did not take no for an answer. 'Yes, sir. I'll come wearing a school uniform next week,' I lied. I don't know why I chose to lie because it made things worse than they already were.

'Ag man, Mafifi! For how long will next week take? Didn't you just say the same thing last week and the week before? Now it's even nearing the end of the year.' The principal was furious; he talked while beating the table with his huge fist. 'But sir, my mother just died and she was the one who was supposed to buy a uniform, I...' 'Stop it, stop! How long are you going to use your mother's death as an excuse? I know you have a father who works, he could always pick up from where your mother left. You should know you are not the only one who lost a parent in this school; the Legodis lost their father, but don't they wear their uniform every single day?' The principal was just comparing the incomparable. How could he compare the Mafifis and Legodis? For Goodness' sake, the people owned three supermarkets and there was no way the death of their father could affect their education. We depended on a salary of one parent who just died, everything was done by mom. She was more like a father and a mother to us, she played both roles. 'You will tell your father that we need a proper school uniform and when he has bought you one, you can come back to school. You have been expelled for now!' The words came as a shock. I had to be at school. It was towards the end of the year and we were about to write our final year examination. I couldn't afford to fail. I had to go to university next year. 'But, principal, I…' I was just trying my luck; I knew I couldn't get away with that one. 'Go home, Mafifi. Come back when you have a uniform. You can leave my office now!' Those were the headmaster's last words and they were final. There was nothing I could do except leave. What a horrible way to start a week. Thank goodness for yesterday's sermon, otherwise I would have collapsed in the principal's office. I sat outside next to the staff room. I wanted to cry but there were no enough tears for what I felt. I was writing mathematics final exam on Wednesday and I couldn't be there. My future is doomed. It is over, I thought. I wanted to give up but the preacher's words kept ringing in my mind: 'Do not worry; let God do the worrying for you…'

'Dikeledi, why are you not in the classroom? People are revising mathematics. Aren't you writing on Wednesday?' my English teacher asked, after finding me seated next to the staff room. Ma'am Masenya was the most understanding teacher I ever knew, always patient and caring.

'What is it, my girl? You look worried. What's bothering you?' she said, grabbing my hand. 'Come on, get up and follow me to the staff room.' I thanked God that there was no one in the staff room. Our school teachers were so inquisitive; they always wanted to know everything about everyone, so they could have something to keep their tongues rolling. 'Come on, tell me, did any one insult you? Was it those silly boys in your classroom? I know it's always one case after the other with them. Go call whoever troubled you, now!'

'No, Ma'am, it's not them. I'm just troubled by my conversation with the principal.' I noticed her eyebrows got raised and then she curiously asked, 'What did Mr Morema say to you, Dikeledi?'

'He said I should go home and come back when I have a school uniform,' I replied.

'Oh, I see…' she said, scratching her head, a sign that told me she was either thinking hard or speechless. 'Can't you ask daddy to buy it for you? At least by tomorrow and if he can't, you could ask him money, you give it to me and I'll buy it for you since I live in town. Will you do that, my girl?' She was just a concerned teacher who didn't know what was happening behind the scenes.

'Um…' I murmured.

'Talk to me, girl. If you don't talk I won't know how to help you.' I decided to break the ice. Don't get me wrong, I'm not that kind of person who goes around badmouthing her parents, I was left with no choice.

'You see, Ma'am, I can't tell dad because I already did that

36

and I just achieved nothing. He always complains about everything, so asking him for money will be useless.' That must have come as a shock to her. She just stood there for minutes without saying a word. I never talked openly about my troubles, not to anyone. After a few minutes of total silence, Ma'am said, 'Did you tell the principal that, Dikeledi?'

'No, Ma'am, I don't think he'll listen. I tried telling him about mom's death and he just told me I'm not the only one who lost her parents.' I slowly felt anger occupy me. 'He compared me to the Legodi family, Ma'am, and we are not even the same and we can never be! They are rich and we...' I paused to catch my breath. 'We, Ma'am, are poor and I think everyone is aware of that!' I fumed with anger.

'It's okay...It's alright...' she said, patting my back. 'It's not like the principal does not care about you. It's just that he deals with a lot of you, and some of you, trust me, they just don't want to buy a uniform. They think it's cool not to wear a school uniform. Tell me if I'm lying when I say that.' She stared at me expecting a convenient answer. 'It's true, but Ma'am I'm not one of them. I'll die to have a school uniform,' I replied, this time with tears in my eyes. She was right; there were others who thought it was cool not to wear a school uniform. It was just their excuse to come to school wearing their "Swagger American boots and jerseys", so they call them. Unfortunately, I had to wear my worn out green jersey which everyone ridiculed. 'So tell the principal that.'

'I can't, Ma'am.'

'Why can't you, Dikeledi?'

'Because he'll never believe anything I say.'

'Then he won't know whether you are part of the "cool group" or not,' Mrs Masenya paused for a second and then she said, 'Okay, go home. I'll talk to the principal. You come write mathematics on Wednesday.' I nodded and left the school premises. When I arrive home I found dad and his lover sitting in the shadow of the shack. They were eating porridge and meat. They must have been delicious because my father couldn't stop licking his fingers. 'You are a good cook, mogatsaka (my love). I never tasted such good food in my life.' Dad's words were an insult to mom. If the dead could hear, I was sure mom was not going to be pleased with him.

'Good afternoon, dad and Aunt Ruth,' I greeted humbly.

'You are back early today. Are those lazy teachers of yours finished with the syllabus yet?' dad asked, busy licking his fingers. 'It's been long that we were done, dad. We are even starting with the final examinations on Wednesday…' I sighed, and then continued, 'Dad, I was expelled from school.'

'Oh, what did you do? Did you play naughty, girl? I know that arrogant principal of yours is very strict,' dad said ignorantly.

'No, dad, I was expelled because I lack a school uniform.'

'Oh, really? I always knew that principal of yours was foolish. What does education have to do with clothing? That just confirms what I always tell you; education is useless, my girl. If I were you I'll start looking for a job.' That was my father, I knew him well, and nothing was ever serious to him. 'Dad, that is not true. Education is the key to a good life. Mom always wanted us to be educated.' I hoped to get his attention.

'Ag man! Wake up, little girl, your mother was illiterate. She did not even know how to spell her own name, yet you tell me about her wanting you to be educated. Stop nagging me with your nonsense and take these plates into the house!' Then that was the end of our short conversation, there was nothing more I could say or do, dad's words were final. When my father was done, nobody dared to continue; it had to be just a yes and amen. I quietly picked the plates and went inside the house. There I found the biggest travel bag I had ever seen. I knew it was Aunt Ruth's, she finally moved in and there was nothing I could do. As I walked around the shack, I realized the cardboard box that was often used as a rack was full with different kinds of food. I bend down to take a closer range and all sort of food were there: peanut butter, oil, margarine, rice... I didn't remember when was the last time we ate rice. We usually ate it on Christmas days or on the first day of a new year. There were just lots and lots of food and some box caught my eye. It was a beautifully designed box written "Weetbix". I never saw that before and I was curious to see what was inside. Excitement started feeling my belly. I was happy that dad had finally decided to buy us food; at least we would rest from porridge mixed with water, that's what I thought until Aunt Ruth opened the door, and started screaming at me like a lunatic. 'Hey you piece of rubbish, take those filthy hands off my food! You are not allowed to touch anything except the bag of mealie meal I found in there!' She scared the hell out of me and I quickly dropped the box back into the cardboard box.

'What is going on here? Dikeledi, I hope you are not bothering your aunt yet, because I won't tolerate such behaviour in my house!' dad said sharply, as he too appeared at the door like a ghost.

'No, no, dad. I was just...' I couldn't finish talking, not while the queen was still alive.

'Shh, shut that filthy mouth of yours!' She turned to my father and said, 'This little rat here was about to eat my food. I was lucky to get here before she finishes everything.'

Those were Aunt Ruth's green lies, and her lies got me kicked hard on my left rib. I thought my rib was broken because of the sound it made when my father kicked it. For Goodness' sake, I was just observing the beauty of the box and I nearly got killed for that. After the queen had spoken those dirty lies, my father ran towards me in a lightning speed, and I covered my face not knowing that this time the target was my ribs.

'If I ever, I mean ever hear your aunt complaining about you again, God help me, I'll kill you with these bare hands of mine!' dad said, squeezing his fists. 'I bought that grocery for your aunt and no one should dare touch it. Am I clear?' I nodded, scared to be kicked like that again. 'Come on, get up and wash those dishes, and make sure everything is clean!' Aunty Ruth screamed at me. I tried to move but couldn't because my ribs were painful, but I forced myself up, took the bucket and left to fetch water. Then I started limping like an injured springbok. I reached

Regina's place and found her mom seated outside. When she saw me coming through the gate, she stood up and ran towards me. 'What happened? Why are you limping, what is it?' She tried helping me walk, instead she held me at the wrong place, the place that hurt the most and I groaned with pain. Then she lifted my shirt and screamed in shock. 'What happened to you, Dikeledi? Who did this to you?' I burst into tears and said nothing. I was not going to tell her that my dad did that to me, that could get me into big trouble. 'Come on, give me the bucket,' she said, grabbing the bucket that was in my hands. 'Let's get inside so that I can find a soothing medicine for you.' We went into the house and she helped me sit on the couch. She then brought a bucket of hot water and dipped a cloth in to rub on the injury. After she was done, she used some ointment written "quick pain reliever" on the injury. It really helped, I felt a lot better after applying it. 'You will take this, and rub it twice on the injury every day.' Mama Regina sounded like a doctor giving a patient a prescription. I felt guilty of finishing her medicines, last time when my eye was hurt; she gave some to take home with. 'But I still have the one you gave me that day, I could always use it,' I said, trying to remove the guilt. 'Don't be silly, Dikeledi. Take this one; it works better than that one I gave you,' she said, putting it inside my pocket.

'You are right. It really works, I feel a lot better now,' I said cheerfully. 'Can I go fetch water now?'

'Yes, you may go kid and please stay out of trouble.' What really fascinated me about Mama Regina was that she was not inquisitive like other women; she didn't get her nose into other people's business. I never told her who had been hurting me all this time, but she never pushed me to let her know. She just asks once and if I choose to keep quiet, she let it go. 'Thank you, Mama, I'm really grateful,' I said with a smile.

'It's fine, baby. Go well.' She opened the door for me as we say our goodbyes. I quickly fetched water and hurried back home.

5

That day I've been trying to dodge had finally arrived. I could do nothing but to go to school and face the headmaster, still with no uniform. Yesterday I did not go anywhere; I just lay down hoping the next day never comes. Unfortunately, it was not in my account to stop days from coming, only The Most High has the final say. Besides stopping the days, I had to write mathematics final exam and I couldn't miss it for anything. I reluctantly dragged myself out of the urine smelling blankets. I hated the fact that my little sister was a bedwetter; it gave me a daily duty. I had to hang the blankets on the line every single day of my life, even on bad days like this. Moreover, I couldn't get used to the bad smell on them, not talking of having to wake up wet and smelly, which was a lot worse in cold days. I gave up on my little sister, I tried waking her up at night before she loses herself, but I was always late. I made fire and bathed Naledi, then myself. I put on my blue skirt, black socks, which I wished were blue and then my khaki shirt, hoping it magically turned yellow. How much I wished I had a full school uniform. That would have saved my mind from focusing a lot on lack of proper uniform while I was supposed to focus on the exams. I also wished to look good in a tie and a pullover. I fantasized a lot about that, imagined myself wearing school tracksuits in winter, because seriously in winter you would feel pity for me. I usually put on my green jersey and when I reach the school gates, I took it off and would freeze the whole day. Sometimes I wouldn't take it off because it would be icy cold. I'll sneak around the whole day hoping the principal does not see me. I dropped Naledi at her school and went to mine, praying that Ma'am Masenya was able to convince the principal or else I wasn't writing my final exams. I entered the classroom and went straight to the back, something I never did in my entire school days. I usually sat in the front row because that was where I got to hear everything the teachers were teaching. The back was usually known for the bad boys in our classroom, and no girl dared to sit there. I arrived early and chose a corner at the back. That was my way of hiding from the headmaster. I was prepared to face the consequences of taking the seat of the bullies than being chased away from school during the exams. I prepared myself for a better future by remembering my brother's words: "Do what you have to do." If it meant being bullied around, so be it! When everyone entered the classroom, they stared at me as if I was crazy; some even pointed at me and giggled. It got worse when

44

the kings of the palace got to their place and found that I had occupied it. I was asked whether I was crazy or looking for trouble. I just gazed at them like someone who was caught stealing. They started making all sorts of silly jokes about me, and everybody burst into laughter. You could hear that they had been holding the laughter for long just by the way it burst out. It got really noisy in the classroom, as everyone was making fun of me and I cared less. I was used to a lot of pain that could never be compared to being bullied by naive learners.

'What's going on in here? What is all this noise for?' Mrs Maredi snapped as she entered the classroom. 'You are supposed to be preparing for the exam but you are busy laughing!' She then pointed at one of the girls who just gathered around another's desk to gossip.

'Zanelle, let's share the joke!' The girl she was talking to was now blinking her eyes constantly as though there was a fly in them disturbing her sight. The party was now over.

'Come on, Zanelle, don't waste my time. Tell us what is so funny since I found you laughing like a mad person!' Then Ma'am Maredi turned around and started searching with her eyes. She focused a lot on the front row, and when she couldn't see what she was searching for, she shouted, 'Dikeledi, where is Dikeledi?' I tried hiding; I don't know why I did that because it got me into a lot of trouble. 'Is Dikeledi here people?' My heart started beating faster. I stood up slowly and shyly said, 'Yes, Ma'am. I'm here.'

'Oh, I see. That is why there is so much noise,' Ma'am said, clicking her tongue disgustingly. 'What is up with you kids? Are you aware that you are writing today? I swear if you fail this exam, there will be hell to pay!' Mathematics was her subject; she taught it from Grade 8 to 12. She was really upset with the classroom disorder. We were supposed to be focusing on the exam that will be coming in a few minutes. 'You!' she pointed at me. 'Get up and go to Mr Morema's office, he's waiting for you.' Those words distracted me, I froze for a while. After a whole minute of not reacting to the call, I came to my senses and started walking towards the door. As I approached the door, I heard Ma'am say, 'Just look at her, she's not even wearing a proper school uniform, yet she makes a havoc in the classroom.' I felt like running and never come back, but I told myself that I have to be strong. I knocked on the principal's office door and a sharp voice said, 'Come in!' I fearfully opened the door and I was ready to beg him to at least let me write the exam when he said, 'Oh, it is you little Miss Mafifi. Today it's your lucky day.' I got surprised by his response, but on the other hand it made me a bit unsettled. I wondered what he really meant by that. 'Ma'am Masenya begged on your behalf. She asked me to let you write this week's exams. She told me by next week you will be having a uniform. I decided to give you this last chance and if next week you don't have a uniform, don't bother to come write other exams. Am I understood?' And I answered with a trembling voice, 'Yes, sir.' To tell the truth I did not understand a thing. I never promised Ma'am Masenya that I would come wearing a uniform next week. I wondered where she got the idea from but I had to admit, the idea was relieving. At least now I would focus more on my exams without the fear of being chased home. 'You may go now,' the school principal said, busy paging one of the big files which were on his table.

'Thank you, sir,' I said, opening the door quickly and left for the staff room. I had to find Mrs Masenya and ask why she told the principal that. I knocked on the staff room door. 'Come in,' a calm voice answered this time. It was Mr Masebe, the physical science teacher. He never taught me but I respected him a lot. He was well-known for his good production. He really knew his work and was passionate about it. He received trophies each year for being the best physical science teacher in the whole district and I admired him for that. He made me wish I was part of the Science stream, but I totally adored commerce and I was good in numbers.

'Yes, how can I help you, young lady?' he asked, busy typing on his computer.

'Morning, sir. Is Ma'am Masenya here?' That was a stupid question; of course I saw that she was not there, since he was alone in the room. I guess I was just nervous and God knew why. I thought Mr Masebe knew why I was looking for her. I know that sounds stupid, but you know that if you do something bad you sometimes feel like the whole world knows what you did. That was how I felt around every teacher at school. I thought they were all aware of me being troublesome by not wearing a uniform. 'No, she won't be here for the whole week but she'll be coming next week.' What? I whispered to myself. She must come back early to take me out of this frustration. I am finished, even the teachers betray me, that's what I thought. I slowly walked towards the door, opened it and went out. Then I went back to the classroom and found everyone quietly seated, waiting for the question paper. I sat at my desk and deeply sighed. Just after a few seconds of sitting, we were given the mathematics paper and told to start writing. I looked at the first question and was totally blank, not because I did not know a thing, but I was mentally disturbed. Fear was threatening my future. "Life is a choice. You do it for you, not for dad, nor for mom. I know you will make it, just hang in there." I didn't know why my mind started singing the words to me but it really helped. Somehow my brother's words cheered me up. The question paper got clearer and clearer as I continue reciting the words.

'No! No! No! Don't touch that,' I said, rebuking Naledi from taking one of Aunt Ruth's apples, which were placed in a bowl on the table.

'But why, sis? I want one, please…' Naledi begged.

'Because I say so!' I rudely replied, trying to scare her from asking further questions.

'But, sis…'

'No, Naledi. You can't have one and please stop nagging me!'

'But Aunt Ruth ate one, why can't I…' Naledi was not ready to give up and that made me a bit angry.

'Hey, you stop that, okay? Stop being a brat!' I shouted at her, to tell the truth, what I did was not necessary. I guess I was just angry that we were not allowed to eat food that was bought by our own father while a stranger from nowhere could. It was bad that I even took the anger on my little sister, and it was the first time she saw me reacting crazily, I really scared her. She ran to the corner of the shack and started crying. I guiltily went there and comforted her. 'Hey…Sis is sorry, baby girl. I should have never shouted at you like that,' I said softly. 'You see, it's just that we can't eat the apples…'

'But why…' Naledi asked sobbing.

'You see… They are Aunt Ruth's…she's sick and the doctor told her to eat lots of apples. If we eat them, they'll get finished and Aunt Ruth will get sick again.' What could I have done? I had no choice but to plot a green lie. I could not have told her the truth because it would definitely damage her innocent mind. She was too little and I had to protect her. 'We don't want Aunty to get sick, do we?' I asked.

'No,' she replied. I wiped her tears off with the tips of my fingers and said, 'I'll bring you an apple from school, okay baby?'

'Okay,' she nodded. I don't know why I made such a big promise because I didn't even have one cent in my pocket. I was not writing any exam today so I decided not to go to school and revise economics at home. We were to write it the following day. I also let Naledi skip school. It was towards the end of the year and they usually did nothing during this time except go to school, play for the whole day and get dirty. I revised economics for the whole day. I was able to memorize all eight essays and was pretty sure that if one of them showed up on the exam paper, I'll definitely "vomit" it.

'Have you two rats been tempering with my apples?' Aunt Ruth asked, after closing the door. She had left with dad in the morning and God knew where she was going. I don't know whether she found it fun to accompany dad to the bus stop every day, or was it just her way of showing off? They would go there hands around each other's waists as if they were teenagers who just started dating. Since Aunt Ruth lived with us, my father has been sleeping at home every single day. Even his drinking habit had changed. He occasionally went to the shebeen.

'No, Aunty, no one touched your apples,' I said apologetically.

'Then why is it like they are not well packed as I left them.'
Really? Did she have to monitor the apples?

'I'm telling the truth, Aunty. We won't dare touch your apples, please believe me,' I begged. I was scared she'll tell dad and I would be in trouble.

'I hope so. I know you little rats never give up; you are always looking for something to tear up with those dirty teeth of yours,' she said, taking one of the apples from the bowl.

'Aunty, I won't eat your apples because I don't want you to get sick. If I eat you will get sick.' I felt like breaking Naledi's little neck for saying that, kids will always be kids, they are so naive. Now I'll have to pay for what she said. 'What is this little rat saying? What do you mean when you say I'll get sick? Have you two witches tried to work your magic on me? Answer me!' Aunt Ruth shouted furiously.

'No, Aunty, you know how kids are, they…'

'Shut up you little witch! I knew I couldn't trust you. Get

out of my face and quickly make fire, I want to bath.' She violently pushed me and I was glad it ended that way, otherwise it could get worse. I comforted Naledi as I was busy making fire. She was disturbed by Aunt Ruth's reaction. When the water got warm, I poured it in a basin and gave it to her. 'You witches may go out now. I want to take a bath!' she said, throwing her bathing towel in the basin. Yes, we had to go out each time an elder took a bath, it was a routine we were used to. Even when mom was still alive that was how it worked except she politely asked us to go outside. We gladly went out and left the madam of the house to shower. When she was done, she shouted that I come take the basin outside. When I went back in, the whole floor was messed up with soapy water and I wiped it while she was busy drawing herself with an eyebrow pencil, and this time it was a grey one. I swear you would find it hard to recognize her when she wakes up, before applying her makeup. Trust me when I say, she overdid it. When she was done "renovating" herself, she left us in peace, and I couldn't care less where she was going.

The next morning I woke up a bit early, I was excited and I did not know why. It was one of those days when I just wake up happy for no reason and it happens once in a blue moon. When I entered the school premises, Ma'am Tjale called me to the staff room. Ma'am Tjale was a good friend of Ma'am Masenya, and she taught us our home language—Sepedi. She gave me a light blue plastic bag and told me it was from Ma'am Masenya. They both lived in town and travelled every day by bus. I took the plastic bag, thanked her and ran to the girls toilets. I got there as fast as a rabbit chased by a hunter, and opened it on the spot. And boom! There it was, a school uniform: a school jersey that was exactly my size, socks and a shirt. I was filled with joy, my heart jumped excitedly. I thought it was a day dream and would soon pass. I pinched myself and yes, it was not a dream, it was real. I put them back into the plastic bag and tied it. I left to write economics with so much joy in my heart, and the same essays I revised early that morning were on the paper. It was definitely my day, I did not just wake up happy for nothing. It was like my freedom day. I felt like a prisoner who had finally served his sentence and was released to face the world once more. I thanked God for the day.

For the first time in my entire school days, I was so excited with a song in my heart because of a new uniform. Though it was not new from the shop, but to me it was as good as new. On that day I received it, I also found a note inside the plastic bag, and it was from Ma'am Masenya. It said I should not be turned down by the uniform because it was not new. She told me it was Rachel's, her niece who matriculated at our school last year. I remembered her quite well and she was my size. That was why the uniform fitted me so well. Ma'am did not get it, people like us didn't care about new or old, all we cared about was our survival. I wore a uniform with pride and looked at myself in a piece of a broken mirror. How much I wished we had a big mirror, which would give me a chance to see myself from head to toe. I walked through the school gates with dignity, and to my surprise I passed the principal's office without fear. I even remembered the pastor's words, in every sermon he preached, he'll always warn us about fear. He told us that God did not give us the spirit of fear but of boldness and of a sound mind. I went to church yesterday and learned a lot. There was no Sunday I could ever miss church because that was one of the places that gave me hope for tomorrow. The only place where I was able to offload my troubles and take my new strength. We were taught about the power of prayer the last Sunday, and thanks to the sermon because some of us never took our time just to say, "Hello, God". I was made aware that we meet God through prayer. We talk to Him when we are sad, even when we are happy. I remembered my mother as a prayerful woman and many times I found her praying especially when she was alone at home. She'll read the bible, sing and pray, and I found that act kind of crazy. I wished my eyes were opened while she was still alive, we could have prayed together…

'Dikeledi, Dikeledi, wait there.' It was Ma'am Masenya, stopping me from entering the classroom. I waited for her to reach were I was, with a huge smile on my face.

'How are you, my girl? I hope you like the uniform. I could see it suits you well, hope you don't mind that it was Rachel's,' Mrs Masenya said.

'Not at all, Ma'am. I quite like it. I don't have to worry that it was Rachel's. It is towards the end of the year and a new uniform would really be a waste. Thank you, Ma'am. I am really grateful.' I couldn't stop smiling and no one would blame me. I was really grateful for people like Mrs

Masenya, she was such an angel.

'Yes, that is what I thought. I could have bought a new one if you were not in Grade 12,' she said, relieved that I understood. 'I am so glad, Ma'am. May God bless you for your kindness and may I not be the last person you help. Thank you.'

'Hmm, I'm sure you are matured enough to go to tertiary. Look how well you speak,' she said with a smile. 'What are you guys writing today?'

'Accounting, Ma'am,' I replied, playing with a calculator that was in my hands.

'Oh, I see. You must be more than ready,' she said, looking at the calculator.

'Yes, Ma'am, I am ready. The time for writing has even arrived,' I said, looking at Mr Lerole who was rushing towards us with a pile of exam papers, he was today's invigilator.

'Come on now, little Miss Mafifi, get inside the classroom. That time has arrived,' Mr Lerole said as he passed us. He was one teacher with a good sense of humour and many learners liked him for that.

'Okay, go on now. Good luck.' Ma'am cheered me up. I thanked her and entered the classroom. Everybody looked at me puzzled. I could read the questions that were written on their faces, "Is that you wearing a proper school uniform?" One of those naughty boys said, 'I wonder where she met the messiah; I bet it was at the dustbins.' Everybody laughed their lungs out and I just didn't care. I had a lot to worry about, like Accounting. I was sure to get an "A" plus on that one. It was one of my favourite subjects and I was not letting a silly joke distract me from succeeding.

6

Five weeks went by too quickly for me. There was only one day left before someone faced the truth. The matric results would be out tomorrow, and truly, that gave me a fright. The so called "Love to be there year" had finally arrived, and my mother was not that lucky to see it. It was a little bit funny because everyone seemed to believe that after the world cup, they'll all be rich and poverty would be a thing of the past. Even the lazy of the laziest believed that. They confidently uttered the same words with a popular television advert, which was played after every five seconds—"2010, love to be there!" My mother usually told me that 2010 would be her year of prosperity and freedom. It was ironically true because now she was finally free. Free from the earth and all its wickedness. I never realized how much I missed her until Christmas day. Aunt Ruth bought all kinds of food you could imagine, used different kinds of recipes to cook, with salads and desserts as accompaniment, but we never tasted even one of the dishes she made. She invited all her friends, from which part of the world they came from, no one knew. They ate every single thing that was there, not leaving a crumb to feed a dog. Naledi and I were told to go play outside and leave grown-ups to catch up. When we return I was told to wash dishes which were all over the place. I swear you would think a party had been going on that day. All I could do was salivate while washing the dishes because of the nice smell that was on them. It was better on New Year's Eve because Mama Regina had invited us to her house, and we really had a great time. For the whole day we were frying meat and drinking a whole lot of cool drinks. At twelve midnight we lit crackers and screamed our lungs out as they made bomb like sounds. We hugged each other as we sang, "Happy new year". I could not help it but cry. I really wished my mother was around so I could hug her, telling her to have a prosperous new year. That was what we used to do while she was still alive. We used to get together at New Year's Eve: me, mom, David, Naledi and dad. That was the only time of the year that brought us together. Even though dad would be so drunk that he would fall down each time he tried to stand. Mom usually forced him to sit but he would arrogantly stand and fall again. Mom usually bought us crackers and snacks during New Year's Eve. She would do everything in her power to make sure that we stayed together as a family on days like that. She believed it was good for family to begin a new year together. She'll send David to the shebeen to bring dad home. But David wouldn't dare bring dad while he was still sober. He usually waited for him to be totally drunk, and then he would drag him home. David too once or twice tried to run away from home on New Year's Eve, to his friends' place, but mom always knew where to find him. Since mom embarrassed him before his "boys", he dared not to run away again. It was a pity that my brother had to spend this New Year's Eve in jail. I missed him a lot, sometimes I cried when I thought about him.

It was now January and just a few hours left before I knew how well I did in my exams. Two things threatened me, the first one was: who was going to help me further my studies if I passed? The second thing was what if I failed? The idea of repeating Grade 12 was a nightmare on its own. In all the threats, at least some voice in my head kept reminding me to have faith, to always hope for good things and never give in. It was going to mid-day and I kept on pulling the urine smelling blankets over my head hoping the day would just pass by. I guess I just happen to forget how bad the blankets smelled because of nervousness. I had never been that nervous in my entire miserable life. I was always the first person to check the newspapers and screamed joyously when seeing how great people did in their matric, and now it was my turn and I just sat there hoping the day passed by.

'Wake up from there, you little brat! Who do you think is going to clean the house and fetch water?' That was Aunt Ruth. I didn't ignore her intentionally, I was still immersed in thoughts and that really got me into trouble.

'You stupid nuisance! How dare you continue lying in those stinking blankets when I'm talking to you? Didn't you hear what I just said?' she said, pulling the blankets with so much power and threw them on the other side of chairs. I sprang up in fear of being beaten up and ran to the door.

'Where do you think you are going, you witch? Come back here!' The woman could scream; it was more like a talent. She did in a way that her rough voice went straight into the ears and blocked them. I got so terrified and started shaking like jelly.

'I...I...I'm going to fetch water, Aunty,' I stammered.

'Water, huh? Where is the bucket then? Are you going to fetch it with those stinking hands of yours?' she said, coming closer. 'Who are you trying to fool, me?' she was beating her gorilla like chest with her gigantic hand. The hand did not look feminine at all. She tried beautifying it with a green nail polish but still... Aunt Ruth was so furious, and I knew if dad was around I would have been dead by now. 'I'm really sorry, Aunty. I'll go fetch water now. It's just that I was thinking about the results that will be out today. You know they make me so nerv...' I could not finish that, not while the drama queen was still alive. 'Hey, hey, hey!' I totally drove her insane. 'You shut up, shut that pipe of yours! I don't want to hear about the stupid results! Are you the first person to matriculate? Who do you think you are? Do you think a moron like you could pass matric? Stop bugging me and go get me water, now!' she said, throwing a bucket at me and I ducked. I quickly dressed and went to fetch water, came back and cleaned the shack, which was upside down. Aunt Ruth was a pure sluggard, terribly lazy. What she excelled in was messing the house up and thereafter give orders. She expected me to do everything for her. Truly, I didn't know what attracted my father to such a woman. She was clearly the opposite of my late mother. I cooked food that I was not even allowed to taste. I usually cooked two pots; one for porridge and the other one for meat. Dad and Aunt Ruth would eat from both pots while we eat from only one, which would be porridge. We ate the usual, a mixture of porridge and water, and if we are lucky enough we would be allowed to eat soup, but meat, NEVER! After I was done with the chores, which included giving Aunt Ruth water to bath, I went to Legodis' supermarkets. I asked dad to give me money to buy a newspaper, but really that was just a trial and error. I knew my father would never give me a cent. The reason for me going to the shops was to find someone who had bought the newspaper and asked them just to have a peep. As I approached the supermarkets, I saw those silly girls from school gathered around the paper, and shouting as they pointed at learners who had passed. When they saw me approaching, they started whispering and I knew they were talking about me, but this time I recognized something different in their eyes—Shame! I started being nervous even though I knew those girls won't be ashamed because I have failed, or maybe they have also failed, and now they were trying to console themselves by gossiping about me. I was surprised when I got there, one of the girls called Sophia, approached me with a crocodile grin and hugged me, and then she said, 'Congrats, girlfriend. You have done well. I bet all teachers are so proud of you, especially Mr Letsoalo and Mr Mamabolo.' I just stared at her wondering what she was on about.

'Sesi (sister) Dike…Sesi Dike,' Regina Mokoena called out to me. She was running towards me with a newspaper in her hands. When she reached where I was standing, she started jumping and screaming childishly. 'You did it. You did! Congrats…'

'Hey, Dikeledi,' said one of the bullies from our classroom, giving me a shallow grin. 'Wow! You are the boss, man. Congrats, man.' He gave me a pat on my shoulder and I, on the other side was still blank. I wondered why I was getting so much attention, even from those people I never imagined talking to me. I quickly grabbed the paper from Regina's hands and started searching for our school, and there I was, written in bold, Dikeledi Mafifi, ACCOH, ECONH… Oh my G-O-D, so screamed my heart. I couldn't believe what my eyes were showing me. I, Dikeledi Mafifi had finally made it. I passed with a university entrance and I was the only one from our school with distinctions, two great distinctions.

The rest passed with university entrances but no distinctions, others just passed and others failed. All those silly girls and bullies failed and only one of the girls passed, and she was standing far away from her friends, as they were busy eyeing her and whispering that she had fooled them. All of a sudden I was surrounded by learners from our school, congratulating me. Some wanted to hug me but others won't let them pass that easily. I was just a celebrity of the moment. I saw some of our classmates seated far from the crowd that was gathered around me, they didn't dare come near, and it was pure jealousy. I did not care. All I could do was code a biblical verse that suited the situation quite well. "O nkabela dijo manaba aka a ntebeletse (He prepares a table before me in the presence of my enemies)". Not everyone would be happy when you succeed. 'Sesi Dike, my dad is calling you. He is over there in the car,' Regina said, pointing at her father's new Polo classic, which was packed not far from where I was standing. Though I was still enjoying the attention, I had to respond to the call. When the crowd heard Regina calling me, they gave me a way. When I got to the car, the door was opened for me and I was told to get in.

'Well done, my child. You have broken the record. We are very proud of you, especially as a community,' Regina's father said, shaking my hand firmly. I wished my mother was there. She would have boasted like a proud mother would. I missed her so much and most of all I missed that motherly love. But I knew she was smiling wherever she was. The car drove off as we left for Regina's home. And there I found a great surprise. Mama Regina had cooked a special meal just for me, and the cool drinks that I saw in the car were bought specially for celebrating my success.

'Congratulations, kid! Your mother would have been so proud of you. You did well, my girl. You did well,' Mama Regina said, brushing my back gently. I spent the whole day there, eating, drinking and laughing. Papa Regina has a good sense of humour. He told us funny stories which happened during his school days. 'I was once called to the staff room for hearing and when I got there, there was no one. I saw a piece of chocolate on one of the teachers' table and I quickly grabbed it, and threw it in my mouth. And when I start chewing it, the teacher entered. That's when I realized that the thing I was chewing had a funny taste. It was a lipstick, and I had no choice but to swallow it quickly because the teacher began speaking to me,' Papa Regina shared the joke.

'I guess when you talked she saw leftovers of her lipstick on your teeth,' Mama Regina teased as we burst into laughter. That was the best day of my life. In the afternoon I went home and of course I wouldn't forget to take a lunch box with me, for my cute little sister. I found dad at home and he was drunk. When he saw me coming, he stood up and staggered towards me.

'My- lovely- daughter. My-lovely-daughter! I am so proud of you, my daughter. O sethunya ngwanaka mane! (you are very intelligent, my child)' He put his heavy hand on my shoulder. 'You see this one, Ruth?' he said, tapping his rough finger on my cheek. 'This is my daughter and she is very intelligent. She topped all those rats at her school, like papa like daughter. This is my daughter...' All I could do was cover my nose with my hands because of the bad smell of traditional beer that came out of his mouth. Besides, he was drowning me with the saliva that was coming out of his mouth as he speaks. 'Here, my beautiful daughter. Go buy yourself cool drink. You have earned it, big time!' Dad gave me twenty rand note. For the first time in my entire life, I received money from my father and that really amazed me. The same person who told me

I won't pass just gave me money to celebrate my success. You should have seen Aunt Ruth; she sat there watching the whole scene without saying anything. She reminded me of a rabbit caught by a snare, she was so embarrassed. She tried removing the shame by constantly scratching her face with her long nails. Then dad started singing a strange invented song as he staggered towards the gate. I laughed as he tripped and fell, thereafter he held the gate tight, helping himself up and then continued with the same song that said, 'My daughter is a genius. She topped all Grade 12 learners, like father like daughter.' I have never seen my father being so happy with anything I've done. I was just scared that he'll brag all the way to the shebeen, and even get into a fight with other men because he will be telling them how dumb their kids were...

The following day my father called me outside the shack, he wanted us to talk, and I wondered what he wanted to talk about.

'Dikeledi, my daughter, we all know how well you have done in your studies, you made me a real man in this village. Now every man respects me and it is all because of you.'

'I am glad to hear that, papa...' I said curiously

'Okay, my point is...you can now get any job you want and with your results, everybody will want to employ you. You can now work at the Legodis' supermarkets.'

'But, papa...' I tried talking but my father interrupted me.

'Don't worry, my daughter. You are probably just nervous and a bit shy, I understand. I'll talk to the Legodis myself.'

'Papa, I don't want to work, I want to go to university. I

want to be a Chartered Accountant, dad!' Before I could say more, dad was already on me.

'What? Chartered Accountant my foot! You must be mad, actually you are insane, little girl! Who do you think is going to waste his money taking you to university, huh?' He shouted like a mad man. If shouting was contagious, I'll say he got it from Aunt Ruth.

'You can get any job you want, but you still want to waste money on a stupid university. Don't you know people go there and still end up useless without jobs? You ungrateful little brat. I swear you will take yourself to university. I don't have money to play merry go round!' That was it. I knew I wasn't getting any more money from him; the twenty rand note was the first and the last money I'll ever get from my father. I knew what I wanted and I was not settling for less, no matter the cost. If it meant losing my father's love, so be it! Besides, there was no love to lose anyway.

7

'David Mafifi, yes, Sergeant, David Mafifi. May you please bring him up here? Someone is here to see him,' said a cop with a huge rough voice, over the phone. I was at the police station, in that same room I waited the last time I came with Uncle Nick, but this time I did not bring company, I was alone. I got fed up because of what my father said and I needed to talk to someone who would understand me, and that person was David. After my conversation with dad, I caught a taxi to the police station, with the same twenty rand note he gave me. Thank goodness, the note was enough for the taxi fare. 'It is you, my little sister. What brings you here?' my brother's voice interrupted my thoughts. I did not see him entering this time, I was still thinking about my conversation with my father. I looked up and saw my brother. It's been eight full months and he had changed a lot. He looked a lot thinner and darker. I swear you could see his cheek bones, and his mouth looked like it was burned with charcoal. He had a lot of scars on his face and hands. I tried to hold back the tears that filled my eyes, but it had not been for long until they ran down my cheeks uncontrollably. David hugged me for a long time without talking, and then he wiped off my tears with the tips of his fingers. 'You must stay strong, Dikeledi, a whole lot is waiting for you out there.' It was as if he knew that I was on my way to "out there". If there was someone who had faith in me, that person was my brother. He always saw this other person in me that I wasn't aware of, and that was the reason why I liked talking to him when I lost hope.

'What really brings you here? I do not like this place for you, you know. This is not the place for you,' David said. I searched in my pocket and took out a page with matric results, which I had torn from the newspaper. The page was having our results and of few other schools.

'What is this? I hope it's not dad on the front page because I know he is capable of scratching out blood,' David joked as he unfolded the paper. I saw his eyes grow wider and then followed a huge smile. My brother stood up and shook both my hands. 'Well done, little sis. I am so proud of you. I always knew there was a dynamite hidden somewhere inside of you. Well done, my little sister. Well done!' I saw tears of joy formed in David's eyes. 'Buti, I don't know where to go from here. You know I really need to go to university and dad says I must go and work as a cashier at the Legodis' supermarkets.' After saying that, I saw David's face changing. The huge smile slowly faded away and replaced by bloodshot eyes. 'Didn't I tell you not to listen to that hard-headed father of yours? I could not further my studies because I listened to what he said and look at me today...' he paused for seconds, caught his breath, and then he calmly said, 'Dikeledi, don't allow anyone to decide on your destiny. You are the only person who is responsible for your own future. You are the pilot of your life; you decide whether your plane crashes on the way or reaches its destination.' 'But, buti, where can anyone go without money?' I asked. 'You are going to do what you have to do. It is your future, remember? Do you want to end up like me, huh? Just look at me, I have no hope, no future, but you do, girl. You are very intelligent, very smart and that is what's required to get there. With these results you can go anywhere. All you need is the right information. Go to your teachers and ask them what to do. I am sure they will not want to see their good product wasted.' What a genius. David was right, I needed to talk to someone with information, someone understanding like Mrs Masenya. She would surely come up with something that could be of help. I had to go and fetch my statement from school the next day and that was my chance of talking to her.

'Thank you, my brother. It really helped talking to you,' I said with a smile.

'I'm glad it did and hoping you know what to do now?' 'Yes, I do!' I said cheerfully.

'Alright then, you have to go now. Our time is up,' David said, giving me a thin smile, and thereafter his facial expression changed to a serious one, and I knew I was not going to like what he was about to say.

'Please, Dikeledi, do not come here anymore, this place is not good for you.'

'But, buti…'

'No, Dikeledi! I am serious about this.'

'So how am I supposed to talk to you when I need to?' I asked sadly.

'Okay, I can only allow you to come back on one condition.' I smiled when I hear him say that. I was prepared to take any condition as long as it meant seeing my brother as often as possible. I smiled and said, 'Anything, buti, anything.'

'You go to university, get your degree, then come back to see me. Deal?' That came as a big shock.

'No, buti! That is not fair. Do you mean I can't see you for so many years? Never!' I screamed in disbelief.

'It depends on you; the quicker you get your degree, the quicker you can come back and see me. The longer you stay in varsity, the longer my time to see you is going to be prolonged. So how is it going to be?'

'Fine,' I agreed with my mouth, but my heart was totally disapproving. How could my brother be so cruel?

'Okay, got to go. See you, Miss Chartered Accountant. Come back to me with that degree.' I watched my brother for the last time going back into the lion's den.

The next day I went to school to get my statement and of course getting information from my teachers was my first priority. It was hard not knowing where to go especially with the registrations that would be starting at the universities in a week or so. I missed my mom more in times like this, I felt like a confused lost child. The teacher's staff room was packed with Grade 12 learners; everybody was there to collect what was theirs. When they saw me, they screamed like lunatics, others gave me hugs and others handshakes. 'Congrats, congrats, you are a star!' Those were words uttered by my former classmates, as they pushed each other to get an attention of a "star". It made me feel like a well-known celebrity that everybody was dying to have her autograph. I enjoyed the attention and could not stop smiling. 'Congratulations, my girl! You put us on the map,' Ma'am Masenya said, with a huge smile on her face. She gave me a pat at the back and held my right hand, dragging me out of the mist of learners who gathered around me. 'Come on now, give her a way. It's time for her to see the producers.' She led me to a group of teachers who were busy sorting out the certificates. 'Congratulations, Miss Mafifi! We are so proud of you,' said Mr Mamabolo, my Accounting teacher, and his face was beaming with joy. 'Take this. It is a token of appreciation from me and Mr Letsoalo. We want to thank you for putting us on the map. Mr Letsoalo is not around today, but he is also as much grateful as all of us,' he said, giving me a present that was well wrapped in a beautiful gold cover. All teachers came and congratulated me and wished me all the best in my studies. The last person was the headmaster. 'Well, well, well… If it is not the troublesome Miss Mafifi. Who would have thought what could come out of her,' he said jokingly. 'Well done, child! You deserve the best, my girl. Your father must be very proud of you. He will surely take you to one of the best universities in South Africa. I too would do the same for my intelligent child.' I wished he would just leave dad out of this. The more I hear about him, the sorer my heart becomes. I wished he was here to listen to what real men would do for their best children. How I wished I had a father like my principal, a father who is not scared of what his children might become. I wanted to cry because of what Mr Morema said, instead I forced a smile on my face and said, 'Thank you, sir.' Ma'am Masenya gave me my statement while pointing out for me some of the subjects. 'Look how well you did in all the subjects, they end with level 5. My dear girl, you have showed us that our effort had not been wasted,' she said, brushing my back while the other teachers nodded with smiles.

'Thank you, Mrs Masenya,' I said, looking at the results, and indeed, I did well in all the subjects, quite well that it even shocked me.

'Dikeledi, please wait for me outside. Do not leave without seeing me,' Ma'am Masenya said, giving some of my former classmates their statements.

'Okay, Ma'am.' I turned to the other teachers and said, 'Goodbye everyone and thank you for everything.'

'Goodbye, my girl. Please make us proud when you get to varsity. Do not play while others do. Know what you are there for, get it and come back to us,' one of the teachers gave me a word of advice while others nodded. I waited for Mrs Masenya nervously, I wondered what she wanted to tell me but I was relieved that I'll also get a chance to talk to her like I promised David.

'So what is your father saying? I mean, is he taking you to

university?' Mrs Masenya asked when we were alone outside. I really hated talking bad about my father but I had to tell it like it was so that I could get help. I told her the whole truth and it really came as a shock to her, though she did not say it, it was written all over her face. She was probably asking herself what kind of a father would do that, and who would blame her? Even I did not understand him. I was very happy when she told me she would help me go to university. She told me about the student loan and how it worked. She also told me the first entering students would be registering on Monday, which was four days from now.

'We must go there early in the morning, actually they must find us waiting for them at the door. You must come and sleep at my place on Sunday otherwise you might end up not registering. The queues there are hectic,' she said with a warm smile. 'Come on now, cheer up. You might even get a bursary, your results are outstanding.' Ma'am was right, I needed to lighten up, and that meant getting dad off my head. I could not stop asking myself whether he was going to allow me to go to varsity, the man wanted me to get a job and help him push his hidden agendas. I suspected he needed help in supporting Aunt Ruth and her children. The woman clearly came with huge responsibilities. She didn't have a job, yet she wore expensive clothes. All her bags were made of leather and she had over ten of them. She changed her hairstyle and nails every week. She once told me that her son and daughter were attending one of the expensive private schools in town. My father's money was clearly paying for their fees. It was a shame I could not trust my own father with my future. I had to come up with a plan. I was not telling him about my plan of going to university, otherwise I would regret the day I did that for the rest of life.

'Come on, take this. Use it to come to town on Sunday. You have my numbers. Call me when you get to town,' Mrs Masenya said, giving me a hundred rand note.

'Thanks a lot, Ma'am. I guess I'll see you on Sunday,' I said, putting the money in my pocket. We said our goodbyes and parted. I just smiled all the way home, day dreaming about the university all the way.

'Hey you little witch, where do you think you are going? Don't you dare walk out of that door!' Aunt Ruth caught me tiptoeing to the door, with my schoolbag in my left hand, and in the other hand was Naledi. I had planned this all week long, and getting caught was the last thing on my mind. I woke up before dawn and packed a few clothes in my schoolbag, hoping to run away before Aunt Ruth was awake. I knew she usually heard nothing when she was asleep, you could slap her and she would not feel a thing. I do not know what woke her up this early today; guess it was not my lucky day.

'I'm...I'm...' I could not say a thing except stammer.

'You are what? You think you can fool me, you lizard. Where do you think you are going so early, huh?'

'You see, Aunty... it is agent. I have to go now,' I said, opening the door and dragging Naledi who was still sleepy.

'Come back here you rat! How dare you walk out on me? Who do you think you are? Come back here!' Aunt Ruth snapped, as she watched us run to the gate. Dad will go nuts when he hears about this, but what could I have done? He left me with no choice. I had to do what I had to do to make sure my future was not at stake. Nobody was going to stop me from going to university, nobody! I took Naledi to the Mokoenas' home. I talked to them about this a few days ago and they supported me. Mama Regina was going to look after Naledi just for a few days as I go to university with Ma'am Masenya. I knew it would be a big sin if I left my baby sister with those two monsters at home, they could eat her alive. I took a taxi to town and it was my first time going there, so I was a bit nervous. I always heard people say it's very beautiful there, and I happened to be lucky to have seen it today. There were so many people, all races where there, black, white, green, yellow... I never saw such beauty in my life: nice cars, beautiful people, tall buildings and so much more. I looked for a phone booth and called Mrs Masenya. 'I'm still in a traffic jam, Dikeledi. Just give me a few minutes, I'll be there,' she said over the phone. Indeed, after a few minute, she stopped next to where I was standing, in a beautiful black BMW. I didn't know she had such a nice car because she usually took a bus to work. But who would blame her? I too wouldn't take such a beautiful car to the dusty roads of Molepo. As I was busy talking to Mrs Masenya, I realized that her husband was a rich business man. He was also managing one of our country's biggest mining companies. You should have seen where they lived, more like heaven on earth, I'm telling you. I was told the suburb was one of the best in Limpopo province. The houses in the suburb were bigger than the Legodis thrice. They were double stories with amazing landscapes. I could not stop staring, with my mouth half opened. I was still fantasizing about having a house that looked like those when we reached Mrs Masenya's home. She asked me to take out a remote that was in her handbag. She pressed it and a huge black and gold gate started opening as we drove in. She then pressed another button and one of the four garages opened and she packed the car in. We stepped out and left the garage closing. I had never seen such beauty in my life; the landscaping was like a Garden of Eden. All kinds of flowers were there, lined up in a way that made the place to look like another planet. Then we approached a door that I thought was a big window until Ma'am slid it aside, and we entered the second phase of the mini heaven. The house was more than amazingly huge. It had upstairs, downstairs and a basement, definitely abnormal for us who were used to staying in a house that was used as everything. Ma'am just smiled as she realized that I was staring at almost everything. She held my hand as we went upstairs. She took me to the biggest bedroom which she said I was to sleep in. It was twice bigger than my home. It had one huge window and from there I could see a big blue swimming pool. The bedroom was neatly decorated and every piece in it had its own match. The gigantic bed was covered with pink and white bedding, with so many pillows on it: big, bigger, and small to smallest, well packed in their order. The carpet was cream white with pink roses, everything was just perfect. I had to sleep on the biggest double bed I had ever seen and that to me was like driving my dream car. All my life I had never had a privilege of sleeping on a bed. Only my parents slept on a single bed which was too small for the two of them. When dad was drunk he usually fell on us as he turned during the night. For the first time in my life I slept with fresh smelling blankets, and only God knew the sorts of dreams I had that night. What I saw at the Masenyas' place gave me new dreams. My dream of wanting a house as big as the Legodis vanished and was replaced by a perfect new vision. Before one sees better things than those she usually sees, one thinks beauty is limited to her surroundings. I just realized that the Legodis' house was just as big as the four garages the Masenyas had. I now had better dreams. I now knew it was possible for one to have more than enough and enough is not enough until you have enough.

8

Early in the morning we left for the university, a world which was still a fantasy to me. This time we drove in a red Range Rover. The most comfortable car I've ever been in. It was just a pity the clothes that I was wearing did not match the car's standard. They made me feel like a servant's daughter when we stepped out of the car. The university was like a big city—another world. There were flats everywhere and people were going up and down like ants. I saw people of my own age looking classier than I did. They were wearing labeled clothes and the way they walked told one the value of their shoes; they walked like they were on eggs. As we drove past the gate, Mrs Masenya asked the direction to the admin building. The security guard directed us but I could not get a thing he was saying. There were so many buildings with the same structure, so confusing for me. We arrived at the admin building, filled certain forms and moved from queue to queue. Ma'am was right; the place was tiring with too many students. Luckily, we got there in the morning. Just when I thought we were done, I found out we were just starting. We were referred to the financial aid offices. It was said there I'll know whether I deserved a loan or not. 'Your results are outstanding, young lady. Go to office no 3, you deserve a bursary,' said a man who was wearing a blue shirt with the logo of the university. My heart jumped with joy when I heard that. The idea of a bursary got me ecstatic. Unfortunately, when we got there we also found another queue. Luckily, it was shorter than those we found in the administration building. Two people were helping the students, an average man who smiled more often while the old lady he worked with seemed bored and every little thing irritated her. She shouted at people even if they made silly mistakes; like this boy mistakenly signed at the wrong place, and the woman shouted at him so hard that I saw the poor boy tremble with fear. I kept on praying that someone would go to the woman before me, so that I go to the friendly looking man. Luckily, my prayers were heard, I had to go to the peaceful man. I gave him my results and he started calculating and I had no idea what he was calculating, but after a few minutes he was done. He looked at me with a warm smile and said, 'Your average is a B. You will get a bursary which will cover everything for this year but next year you will have to apply for a student loan,' he gave me back my statement. 'Would you like to know anything else, young girl?'

'No sir, thank you.' There was nothing more to say. I got

a bursary, which meant I was finally in the university. I, Dikeledi Mafifi was finally a student of the University of Limpopo, Turfloop campus. It was more like a dream coming true. I signed some papers which I had to take back to the admin building. Mrs Masenya was so happy when I tell her the good news, she couldn't stop congratulating me. Pity she did not experience the moment herself because I had to go in and leave her outside. We then went back to where we started to get a clearance receipt, a confirmation that I was free to register. Then we went to the school of economics and management sciences, where I registered as a Bcom student. Phew! The procedure there was so hectic. I bet you queue even when you go to the toilets. At last we were done with the registration process, but there was just one little thing left, getting my room keys. The idea made me crazy. I was going to have my own room in the university residence. How cool was that? After getting the keys we went to a cafeteria and got ourselves something to eat. For the whole day we had been queuing and never got a chance to eat. After eating we left to see my room. I had written the name of the residence on a piece of paper, so I wouldn't forget. We asked some guys where the so called VH residence was, and they were so helpful as they took us there. The number of the room was written on the key holder, so we looked for the room and it was found on the third floor. We unlocked the door and went in. It was a double room and it had two single beds, lockers, small shelves, chairs and study tables. It looked like I had a roommate. My mind kept wondering who she was and what she looked like. Guess I'll have to wait and see. I looked outside the window and saw a great view of a pond and a mountain. When I was finally satisfied with viewing the room, we locked and left. It was late in the afternoon when we left the campus so I had to sleep at Bendor Park once more, on the same wonderful bed, which gave me fresh dreams. When we got there I took a hot bath and went straight to bed. It had been a long exhausting day but I was glad it paid off well. As my eyes closed slowly, I wished I was not going back to the dusty Molepo village again.

'You stupid child, today I am going to kill you!' My father's sharp voice terrified me as I slowly closed the shack door. I was hoping they would not be around when I get back, but I was ready to suffer the consequences. 'Where have you been all these days? You think boys play, huh? You don't even respect us anymore. Today I'll show you who I am!' What? Me? Boys? I was totally lost about what my father was saying. Could he really think I would go all the way to see boys? He definitely didn't know me. For crying out loud, I was from Turfloop campus and I've brought good news. I got a bursary. Shouldn't a lady be respected for that? The bursary thing brought a huge smile on my face each time I thought about it, and this time I did not realize I was beaming openly and that really freaked my father out. 'You little bastard! You think this is funny, huh? I am talking to you!' Dad slapped me so hard that I started coughing blood. He was just about to repeat the act when Naledi rushed to him. She quickly grabbed dad's leg and started pulling it.

'No, no, papa! Leave Sesi alone,' Naledi said with teary eyes. She was clearly frustrated by my father's reaction. 'You think this sister of yours is clever, huh? She is a moron. She let boys rob her. I'll kill her today!' dad said, violently pulling his leg away from Naledi. All of a sudden my father cared how I used my femininity or maybe he was just worried that I'm not using it to benefit him. Wasn't he the one who once said I should use my femininity to get myself things?

'No, papa, she did not go for boys. She went to school, school papa, school!' It was the first time my little sister did that, usually when dad was on me, she froze and stayed at the corner crying. 'What school? Oh, I see she lied to you. Don't you know schools are not yet open? Furthermore, your sister is not a scholar anymore. Instead of looking for a job, she runs off with boys!'

'No, school, school, school...' Naledi was not ready to listen to dad's lies. She knew I would never lie to her and that really made my father mad.

'You see, Dikeledi, you see?' he said, pointing at Naledi who was now pulling dad by his jacket. 'You even taught this little rat to disrespect me. Get off me before I kick you!' dad said, pushing Naledi away. Shame, my little sister, it was her way of getting attention. Pity she was not aware of the kind of monster she was dealing with.

'Dad, she is right. I went to the University of Limpopo.' Mentioning the word university made my father go wild. I did not know what made varsity freak him like that. Every time he heard about it, he went nuts.

'What? Do you even know what direction the university is, you lying cow? Just because I never matriculated it does not mean I am stupid. You will tell the truth today or I'll kill you!'

'Dad, I am not lying. I even got a bursary which will be paying for everything this year. I went with Mrs Masenya, I slept at her place, dad. You can even ask her. Here are her numbers,' I said, giving him a piece of paper that was written Mrs Masenya's phone numbers.

'So you have started disrespecting me. You go places without my permission, you even chose yourself new parents,' dad fumed with anger. 'Okay, okay. From now on I disown you as my child. Take whatever is yours and leave my house now!' he said, tearing the piece of paper with phone numbers into tiny pieces.

'But, dad, you were not here when…'

'Shut up! Shut up and leave now!'

'Dad, I am sorry. I won't do it again.'

'Now, Dikeledi! Go before I do something I'll regret.' I knew he meant that well and there was nothing more to do or say that would change his mind, unless I wanted to wait for an ambulance or even the undertaker to take me out of the house. My father pointed at the door, my own father disowned me because I went to look for a brighter future. What kind of a father does that? I picked up the schoolbag that was lying on the floor and left. As I was approaching the gate, I heard tiny footsteps coming behind me. It was my little sister, I forgot all about her. 'Sesi, where are you going? Wait for me, please,' she begged innocently.

'Where are you going? Go back. Dad did not chase you away,' I said, bursting into tears.

'I'm coming with you, Sesi,' Naledi said. I wiped my tears and held my little sister's tiny hand as we went to Regina's home.

'Your father must be crazy. How can he not appreciate the fact that you got a bursary? At least he could just rejoice in that because the burden of paying the fees is off his shoulders,' Mama Regina said, patting my swollen gums with a cotton wool. She was so angry and I even saw her hand trembling as she spoke. 'When are you going to varsity?'

'Next week Monday. We will be starting with the orientations on Tuesday,' I said, drinking a pill she gave me.

'You will have to leave Naledi with us, she can't stay with your father. He'll have to answer to me if he dares show up. He won't like the social workers to get involved in this!' I had never seen Mama Regina so emotional, she was really ready for my father and I wondered what would happen if they met face to face.

'Thank you, Mama. May God bless you for your kindness.'

'It's okay, baby,' she said calmly this time, that was the tone I was used to. 'You know, kid, your mother was a good woman and she loved you. I am doing what she would have done.' She was right; my mother would rather die to have seen us suffer like we do now. I decided to stay at Regina's home until Monday. The following day I went to my home and took all our clothes. Dad was not there, I had to wait for Aunt Ruth to go out first before I go in. Luckily, the door did not lock and never did. We always used a wire to close it when we leave. I took all my tattered clothes and one family photo. I needed something to remind me of the people who mattered the most. Something that will get me going for the next three years, when I'll be away from home. When I closed the door, I started crying. I just realized I was leaving my home, the only place that I was used to, and now I was going somewhere strange. I was going to start a new life and that scared me. Monday morning finally came and I had to say goodbye to everyone and that was the hardest thing I had to do in my entire life. Shame, my little sister could not stop crying, she even ran after me. Mama Regina had to pull her off me when I get on the bus. It was all sad and I also cried. I was going to miss her so much. I was just glad that I was leaving her in good hands; I was sure Mama Regina was going to take a good care of her.

9

The university was still a huge place for me, I couldn't remember how many times I got lost but as often as one could imagine. The taxi dropped me right at the university gate and this time it was a pedestrian gate. It was not the one we used by the time I came with Ma'am Masenya. That day we used a motor gate, I guess.

'Ag man, not again! Not another stupid fresher from *magaeng* (First year student from rural areas). I just get tired of seeing them every year,' said a tall guy of my brother's age. He was looking down at me as if he was a famous American basketball player.

'Mack, you are an old dog maybe you are tired of barking in the university premises!' A certain girl shouted at the guy as she passed by, and her words were spiced with giggles from a group of girls who were with her.

'Hey Maggie, Maggie, you are going to pay for this. I tell you, man!' That tall guy who had been looking down at me a few seconds ago, shouted at the girl who boastfully flung her hair as she walked away. Then the "NBA" player turned to me and said, 'Hey you! Typical rural girl, wake up! This is varsity, not some cow's kraal. Are you going in or out?' The words were followed by an outburst of laughter from a group of guys who were with him, and that woke me up from day dreaming. I realized that I was standing right in the middle of the entrance and blocking a way for people who were passing by. I was still stunned by the campus and trying to figure out which way to take. 'Hey, young girl, step aside! Don't you see you are blocking the way?' a guy wearing a sky blue security uniform rudely shouted at me.

'Sir, I want to go to the residence place…VH, I guess that's the name of the residence. May you please show me the direction?' I humbly asked the same security guy who seemed not interested in what I was saying. 'VH…Sir, do you know where it is?' I repeated myself to get his attention. 'Where is your student card, young girl?' asked another security guy, who was wearing the same uniform. 'Sir? Student card…' I said, trying to figure out what that could be, and then some students arrived and showed the security guards a card that had a picture and names on just before passing. Then I recalled I also got that thing on that day I registered, it must be the student card the security guy wanted. I quickly searched my bag, took out the card and gave it to him.

'Okay, young girl. Go that way, to the northern residence, you will find VH there. It's next to the pond.' I nodded as if I had understood whereas I did not. I took the northern direction, looking at all the sides but I saw nothing. There were so many residences and I did not see any with the name VH. I got in one of the residences and got lost right inside the building. I did not know my way back to the entrance so I kept coming back to the same place while trying to find my way out. Some silly girls noticed that I was lost and they started giggling. I asked them where the entrance was and that was my way of firing their laughter. I wondered what was so funny; they were just amused by a first year student who got lost—how foolish. After a few minutes, when they were satisfied with their stupid laughter, one of them showed me the entrance. I went out and asked a certain girl where VH was, and she pointed at a residence just next to the one I got lost in. I felt like beating myself up. I could not believe I went to such a trouble while the thing I was looking for was right in front of me. I guess they were right when they said "Knowledge is power". I went into my room and threw myself on the bed. I was exhausted from roaming around looking for the so called VH, which was not even written on the building. I wondered how they knew all these residences since there were so many of them that looked alike. After resting for an hour or so, I decided to pack my tattered clothes in the locker, and then I made my bed. I took that one family photo and pasted it on the wall using a chewed bubble gum. I thought I needed to see my family every day; they were my source of inspiration and reminded me of where I came from, and also where I was going. As I was still busy packing, some people got in. It was a girl of my age and two grown-ups, who I assumed to be her parents. She introduced herself as Khensani, my roommate. She was tall and beautiful, and just like her mom, she had dimples. Her mother was a classy type; she looked sophisticated and highly educated. She wore a black skirt, red blouse and matching red high heeled shoes and a black handbag. She was slim, with a coffee coloured skin, a very beautiful black woman. Her father was rather a huge black man with a big belly. He was wearing a black suit with a blue shirt and a matching blue tie. My roommate was just wearing a simple black jean with a white golf shirt and Nike snickers. The family looked rich and organized. I helped them offload her things from her father's Jeep Cherokee. She brought a lot of things for a student; I wondered if they would all fit in her space. There was a plasma TV, DVD, fridge, a small classy couch, her clothes and a whole lot of other stuff. I wished I had parents who cared like hers, parents who would want to see where I would be staying for the next three years. I knew if my mother was alive she would have accompanied me. She wouldn't let me approach my first year at the university like an orphan, just like my father did. After my roommate was done packing her stuff, I felt ashamed. My space looked like a lost piece of another puzzle.

'Khensani, may you please turn the volume down, I am trying to study,' I pleaded with my roommate, who was playing the music in a way that I felt the chair I was sitting on vibrating. I didn't know why she chose to bring friends on a blue Monday; she was literally driving me insane. I told her I was writing a test tomorrow but she sure chose to ignore me. They were some sort of a distraction. They danced all over the place, some of them jumped on the bed and some throwing up on the floor. There were cans of beers all over the floor and so much noise you'll think it's a bar. 'Khensani,' I called out to my roommate who kept on dancing and pretending not to hear me. She was having a time of her life and was not going to let "silly me" distract her. It's been nine months since we've been at varsity but you won't believe me if I told you my roommate never went to attend a single lecture class. She was either out there partying or in the room sleeping. She only went to class when she wrote tests and I did not know how she managed. She was lucky because her parents bought her every single textbook that she needed, she even had study guides but she did not use them. If it was me having all those materials, I would have studied until I turned red. It was nearing the end of the year and I have never seen my roommate going to attend any lecturer. All I knew was a time when she had to write a test; a certain girl would come and tell her they were writing a test the next day, and then she'll leave Khensani with notes and previous question papers. My roommate would give the girl a few bucks and thanking her for being a loyal personal assistant. This other day one of Khensani's friends was mocking her about her issue of trying to bribe a certain lecturer, apparently it did not go well. Seriously? Did she think she could buy her way up? I knew why my roommate was giving me such an attitude. It was because I refused to join their so called "The clamour girls crew".

'Khensani, please, I am talking to you.'

'What? What Miss goody-goody? It's not my fault that you do not have money to spoil yourself. You see this?' Khensani said, pointing at the DVD. 'It's my parent's money and I play it anyhow, and you Miss nice girl can't tell me anything.' Then she continued dancing to the music that was blocking my ear drums.

'Khensani, I just want to study. I told you I am writing a test tomorrow.'

'Ag man, shut up! Are you the first person to write tests? Wake up, little girl, this is varsity not a primary school.'

'Yeah, Dikeledi, you think you are too smart, huh? Leave us to have a nice time since you are still hooked up in the olden days. Just look at the freaking shoes she's wearing, you should let us hook you up with a rich guy so that you can look sophisticated.' Those were Sarah's words, one of Khensani's party friends. What she said did not bother me at all because I knew where it originated. She was just angry that I refused to go out with some guy they brought to me this other day. The guy told me how much he loved me and that he would buy me everything I wanted if I agreed to date him. I wondered why a good looking guy like him seemed so desperate to date a typical rural girl like me. I remembered my mother's advice, she used to say, 'Dikeledi, my girl, you must be wise in this life time. There are people who would come into your life just to destroy you because they are scared of what you would amount to if they let you focus, so avoid them in all circumstances!' I had no idea what mom was talking about until I met the kinds of people I lived with at varsity. I chose to avoid such people and befriended my books. I realized that I was not going to win with the loud noise in the room and gladly picked up my books and went to the library. When I open the door, Khensani said, 'I wonder why you never did that in the first place. That's better than sitting here and waste your time by bossing us around. Weren't you aware of libraries before, girl? It is specially made for sweet little bookworms like you!' I just went out and avoided her. I wasn't letting her take my focus away, I knew where I came from and I was also aware of where I was going. I had a vision and I was not letting people like Khensani distract me. I found a phone booth on my way to the library and called home. Mama Regina's phone rang for a long time without anyone picking it up, and that made me a little bit nervous. When I was about to hang up, she answered. 'Mama Regina, ke Dikeledi, le kae? (It's Dikeledi, how are you?)'

'Oh, hello, my girl. How are you doing? You know we miss you so much and a lot has happened since we last saw you during Easter holidays…'

'What happened? Is my little sister okay?' I panicked.

'Of course, she's alright. Don't worry about her but…'

'Mama Regina, what is it?' I was becoming more and more nervous.

'Your father was here after you have left and he was very angry. He heard that you came home and he even threatened to report us to the police for kidnapping you.'

'What? Papa chased me away, he disowned me. I am very sorry, Mama Regina. I hope he did not cause much trouble.'

'No, not much. He was just shouting and saying we should give Naledi to him.'

'No, he can't take her, Mama Regina. Please don't let him take her. Naledi cannot stay with that abusive woman.'

'Don't worry, my girl. I won't let anything happen to Naledi. Papa Regina sorted him out. He told him he was going to report him to the police for abusing you and that really scared him. We told him that you were ready to testify against him. I do not think he'll be bothering us again.' Then I heard "beep... beep" a sound that warns you if the money is getting finished. I only had two rand that I used to make the call, pity I could not say goodbye to Mama Regina. I did not have a phone where she could get a hold of me, so they usually waited for me to call them. I was just glad that they were able to sort my father out otherwise I wouldn't feel at ease. I knew how troublesome my father could be, and I did not want him to bother the Mokoenas. They were good people and took good care of my little sister. The last time I went home was during Easter holidays. I never saw my father or even bothered going to visit him. My heart was rather sore that I did not see him. I wanted to tell him how well I was doing in my studies, but I was too scared of being choked to death. It made me shiver when I thought of what my father would do to me the next time he saw me. I decided never to go home during holidays. It was a pity that during festive season, they closed the residences and wanted everyone out but I made a plan. I knew I was going to miss my little sister so much, but I needed to make sure that dad and I are in good terms before I visit. I knew my father very well; he was not going to let it go just like that. As long as he hears my name being mentioned, he'll definitely lose it. I was lucky that whoever told him I had come home during Easter holidays, got there late otherwise he would have come and strangled me right in front of the Mokoenas. The further I stay away from home, the lesser the havoc.

10

A full year and a few months passed by without me going home. Mama Regina tried to convince to come back, so many times but she ended giving up. She sent me money to buy a phone so they could at least call me anytime they missed me. I talked with Naledi a lot on the phone, almost every day. We missed each other a lot and sometimes we even shared tears over the phone. The thing that made me to cry more was that she wanted me to come home but I couldn't. I hated telling her I can't come back because it made her really sad. She told me she was doing very well at school; she was even part of the top five in her classroom. Surely she grew up faster than I imagined; I could even hear progress as she speaks. The thing that made me even happier was that she was no longer bed-wetting. I hated the fact that she messed up the Mokoenas' bed. I asked Mama Regina to let her sleep on the floor but she refused. She'll just say, 'No, Dikeledi, I can't do that. It's cold on the floor, God will punish me. It's fine, we can always take the mattress outside to dry it.'

What an angel, I don't know how many women would be so kind to children that were not theirs. The maturity in my little sister's voice told me that years had passed by quicker than I imagined. I was finally in my final year at varsity. It hasn't been easy in the past years but I was glad that I passed every single challenge that was on my way. Last year had not been one of my favourite years because I struggled a lot without food and study material. I tried my best to make sure I study and eat. I used the little money that I got from Mama Regina to buy the necessities. I usually borrowed books and made sure I used the time I had effectively. I was usually given two hours with the books and I made sure that within that time I filled my memory with a lot of stuff. Then I got higher marks than the owners of the books; that's were jealousy arose and they began denying me access to their study materials. But that did not stop me; I went and borrowed from others. During exams I borrowed the books at night and while everyone was fast asleep, I'll wake up and study, and in the morning I'll return the books to their owners. At least this year it had been a little bit better because the student loan gave us a stipend to buy books and grocery. I nearly ate out of dustbins last year. The little that Mama Regina gave me was not enough to last me for the whole month. The poor woman tried her best; she was not working but she made sure she sent me money every month end. Only her husband worked, but she would take money out of the one he had given her and sent it to me. Pity things were so expensive, I only bought two or three things and then the money would be gone. Some days I slept with an empty stomach. One day Mama Regina asked me if the money was enough and I just lied and said it was. I did not want to bother her, she was doing her best and all I could do was to appreciate rather than complain. Luckily, God brought another angel in my life. I met a girl named Sophie, and she was more than a friend to me. She shared with me everything she had and was never a type to complain. I wished I had not been ashamed to tell her about my troubles the first time I met her, otherwise I wouldn't have suffered like I did Last year. I met her at church towards the end of my first year. I've been going to her home during school holidays. Before she knew my troubles I would tell her I was just visiting her home until she finally realized that I was hiding something from her. Then I told her the whole truth about me, and really she understood. She accepted and loved me with all my troubles, and her parents were also warm hearted, they treated me like family. I just thanked God for all the angels he sent in my life. During the past few days I got my results and I have passed all my subjects, which meant I was going to graduate. The idea of graduating excited me so much that every day I woke up at dawn and ran to the stadium. When I got there, I'll go stand in the last row where the pond was a lot clearer, where I could clearly see the top of the residences and the mountain, and when I am up there I'll scream my lungs out, saying, 'I have made it! I, Dikeledi "Silly girl" Mafifi will be graduating soon. That day has finally come. Do you hear me? That day is finally here. Yippee…'

'Hey you, angel. I see you are still on the path of righteous-ness. Yeah man, you will surely go to heaven one day.' Those were Sarah's mockery words as she watched me enter the pedestrian gate. She staggered towards me, not ashamed of smelling like brewery on a white Sunday like this. I was surprised at seeing her. Since we parted in December, in my first year, I never saw her again. I wondered where Khensani was.

'You see us, especially me,' she said, tapping her chest with her finger. 'I will surely go to hell, but I am sure I won't be alone there. I will find your boyfriend Jack there.' She burped right in my face and I felt like pushing her away because of the bad liquor smell that polluted the whole place in just a second. She looked horrible; her hair was a mess. She was holding a bottle of beer in her hand and in the other was a cigarette. It was as if she just woke up at the dumping site. I tried walking away as fast as possible but she kept on following me.

'Well, well, well…look at that skirt. Damn girl, you look good. It's just a pity that you have forgotten all about us. Your ex-roommate is lying there in Mankweng hospital and she is dying. Your boyfriend Jack died but you don't care, do you?' I had no idea what she was on about. At last I decided to open my mouth and ask what she was bugging me for.

'Who died? And who the hell is Jack? What is Khensani doing in hospital?'

'You remember that charming guy we tried to hook you up with? The fool died of AIDS. You see, angel, you did yourself a huge favour by rejecting that bastard, otherwise you will be dead too. Come, come and see...' Sarah said, dragging me to the notice board that was just there by the gate, and she pointed at a photo that was pasted there. I could not believe what I was seeing; it was a photo of that guy I refused to go out with. That good-looking guy who told me how much he liked me, and what he could do for me if I agreed to go out with him. The notice showed his picture, the date of his death and where he will be buried. They did not say much about the cause of his death; they just said it was due to a short term sickness. I felt sorry for him, but on the other hand I thanked God I did not fall for his tricks. Sarah told me that the guy slept with girls so that he could infect them with the virus just because he did not want to die alone. How wicked was that? May God have mercy on him on his judgment day. I realized that I was one of his targets but he failed. I remember Khensani was very angry at me for rejecting a good looking guy like that. I felt sorry for Khensani too. She was such a good girl when I met her, she just allowed herself to be corrupted by bad company. I was overwhelmed by what Sarah said and probably by what I just saw. I left Sarah screaming at everyone that was passing by and telling them how bad AIDS is. She kept on dragging people to the notice board and telling them how foolish Jack was. 'Pamokate ga e raloke bafowetu, (Aids doesn't play, guys)' that's what she kept on saying as she dragged strangers to see Jack's picture.

The next day I decided to pay Khensani a visit at the hospital. When I got there I could not believe what I was seeing. I just held back my tears; it was really painful to see khensani like that. She was lying there, on the hospital bed, helpless. She was very thin, so tiny and her head was just too big for her neck to carry. Her mouth was covered with a white substance and flies could not stop moving around her. She tried to keep them away but her hand was too weak to do that. The girl was so beautiful and healthy when I met her, and now she was lying there, helpless and waiting for death.

'Hi…how are you? I…I heard you were here and thought I should come and check on you,' I chocked. I seriously didn't know what the right words would be for a situation like that. I was so nervous and I wished I could just disappear. I never imagined it to be that bad.

'Who…who are you?' Khensani said, trying to rise up but her head was just too big for her tiny little body to carry. She was too weak and talking seemed like a piece job to her.

'It's me…Dikeledi, remember your first year roommate?' I just couldn't stop the stammering, I was terrified.

'Oh, DI-KE-LE-DI. I am so happy that you came. I always knew you had a heart of an angel. You see, since I got admitted in this hospital, nobody came to see me, not even my parents. They are angry at me and they have disowned me,' she said, coughing and it took long for her to stop. I managed to hold her tiny hand and said, 'It's okay. God loves you. Don't give up.' I gave her a tissue to cough in and I could see blood on it as she wiped her mouth. She was really in pain and I felt weaker as I watched her try to move but she couldn't.

'It's over, Dikeledi. It really hurts that my life is ending like this. I am still young, Dikeledi, and to watch myself die like a helpless dog, it is so painful. But it is my entire fault. I got what I deserved. I should have focused on my studies like you and kept my life busy by going to the library, maybe my life could have turned better. Just look at me now, I'm useless and helpless. I can't do anything except watch myself die.' She started coughing again and this time it got worse. The nurse came and helped her up. She put a pillow behind her to support her tiny little body. The nurse turned to me and said, 'I think you should leave. She needs to rest now.' I nodded and bid her goodbye.

'Dikeledi, I am glad you came to see me, your visit really meant a lot. Thank you.' Khensani managed to say those words and she really touched my heart. I gave her a pat on the back and left. I was traumatized by what I saw. I never saw something like that in my entire life. It really killed me that such a young person could die so helpless. I felt a little bit sick and I went straight to my room, and when I got there, I just threw myself on the bed and slept. I even had a nightmare where Khensani was walking in the streets naked, and her tiny body being eaten by worms. A week later, I met Sarah again but she was sober this time. She told me bad news; Khensani had died. My heart sank with sorrow. The same feeling I felt when I heard my mother died overshadowed me. I was about to faint when Sarah held me and supported my body as we walked to my room. We found Sophie lying on the bed, reading her favourite novel. We were staying together in our final year. When Sophie saw Sarah helping me into the room, she threw the book aside and rushed towards us. She was so sad when I told her what happened. Sophie was more than a friend to me, she was like a sister I never had. We talked about everything. She knew everything about me and it was the same with me. She was so soft at heart, understanding and loving. I felt so lucky to have met her.

11

It was now a new year and even more exciting because I'll be graduating tomorrow. I could not describe how excited I was. It was more than an excitement. It was twice the feeling I had when I matriculated. I felt like small bubbles were moving in my belly. I never went home during December holidays instead I went to Sophie's home. I spent the rest of the holidays there and never felt a little bit of guilt attacking me. Her parents were the nicest people I knew and they treated me like one of their own. Mama Regina just gave up on me, she tried to talk to me about coming home but I refused. I just couldn't believe the fear of my father was still there even after a full three years of not seeing him. I was just happy that it was only fear that was left; the anger had evaporated into thin air. I actually found it in my heart to forgive my father and I was not sure if he had forgiven me. I missed my little sister so much, and I could not wait to see her tomorrow. She would come with Regina's family for my graduation. I was even glad that I would have more than enough time to see them before graduating because they promised to come early in the morning. The reason being they had my academic regalia. Mama Regina promised to buy me the regalia and "thank you" was not enough for such angels. I do not know how many times I put on Sophie's regalia, but still I was not satisfied. Sophie and I wore the same size, so her regalia fitted me well. The feeling of walking on a red carpet and getting my degree got me running wild. Sophie walked in as I was pretending to be a queen, walking towards the mirror with her regalia. When she saw me she smiled and said, 'You sure must me tired. You've been doing that all day. Come on now, It's time to rest.' she pulled me by my hand, and threw me on the bed. I just giggled and took off the regalia. She was right, I was tired. Since she left for the university in the morning, I never took it off.

'Here,' she said, giving me some folded paper.

'What is it?' I curiously asked.

'Just open it, you will find out,' Sophie said, kicking her shoes off, and recklessly throwing herself on the bed. She also looked tired. She left in the morning to fix her file and just came back now. Her names were not in order, so she had to fix them before the graduation day. I took the paper and unfolded it. It was a letter.

Hi Dikeledi

I hope you are well. I know you must be excited since you are graduating tomorrow. I am so happy for you. You know I have been looking for you for a while. Luckily, I saw your friend today. I just wanted to appreciate what you have done. You know your life is a living testimony. Truly, you are an inspiration. You made me to look at life with a different eye. I also have a background like yours. My parents died while I was still a kid, and my brother and I were left with my father's sister who abused us. Unlike you I decided to live recklessly and I blamed everyone for my life. I thank God for people like you who had showed us that life is a choice. I have decided to turn my life around. I study hard now and even visit church once or twice. Just like you, I also want to be a better person. I hear you've been hired to start working at some accounting firm. Congrats, and thanks for showing us that there is still hope.

Sarah

I did not realize that tears were running down my cheeks until Sophie gave me a tissue. They were tears of joy. My success was impacting people's lives and that was another success on its own. I was happy that there were people who were inspired by my life, and that really made me feel useful. I was really proud of Sarah. Who would have thought people like her could look up to a typical rural girl like me? I smiled all the way to my bed and I had the most beautiful dream ever. Before the cock crowed, I was awake. It was that day, the day I've been dreaming of, the best day of my life. A smile wouldn't be enough for a lovely day like this. I just thought maybe giggling would do better. I waited at the gate impatiently for the Mokoena family to arrive. I gave them the direction to Sophie's home and hoped they would get it right. I couldn't afford that they get lost on a special day like this, especially with my regalia. Sophie's place was in Toronto, the township next to the university, so getting lost was just not guaranteed. I waited at the gate nervously, wondering how big my little sister was. I had missed much of her growing up in the past three years and I was not proud of that. I missed her so much and could not wait to see her, and everybody else. I was still fantasizing about how everybody looked like now when a taxi stopped at the gate. It was them, they finally arrived. My heart started pumping faster than usual, I was very nervous. Papa Regina was driving and I knew he must have bought a new taxi this time. It was a fifteen-seater, red in colour, with dimmed window panes. I wouldn't have known it was him if he hadn't opened the driver's window. The man was prosperous; he always had something to show for his hard work, compared to other men. How much I wished I had a father like him. He loved his family and protected them in all ways. I just wondered why they came by a vehicle with that much capacity while it was just a few of them. I was expecting only four people, unless they decided to bring the whole village along with them. I gave Mama Regina a big smile as she walked towards me. She looked a little bit older than I saw her three years ago but that warm smile was still fresh as ever. She hugged me for a few minutes without saying anything and I could feel that I was really missed. After what seemed like a decade she managed to say, 'We missed you a lot, child. Well done! You've made us very proud.' She had tears in her eyes, tears of a proud mother. Before I could say anything, Regina and Naledi were dragging me back and forth. They were so happy, more like they had just gone insane. They kept on screaming and I could not get one word they were saying. They were competing to get my attention. They wanted to tell me everything that happened during the past three years in one minute. Luckily, Papa Regina saved me from their competition, which was beginning to stress me out as I could not catch a thing they were saying.

'Hey, hey, quiet, kids. We don't want to give your sister a headache on this wonderful day. Keep that for later, alright?' Papa Regina said, as he firmly shook my hand with a huge smile. 'These two are just a pain in the neck. It has always been like that for the past three years. Well done, my girl. We are very proud of you.' He was also aging, the grey hair that I saw three years ago, starting to grow, had just covered half of his head. That was one man you wouldn't mind getting older because he played his role very well during the days of his life. My little sister was very neat and lovely. I could see she had been getting more than a proper care. She had grown to be a beautiful young lady. She had mom's big eyes and was taller than last time I saw her. I was glad that she and Regina were like sisters. They reminded me of our early childhood, during those times when David and I used to fight for little things. We competed in getting mom's attention but we never stopped protecting each other. I heard that if anyone would beat Naledi at school they were to face Regina after school. Regina reminded me of David, they were the kinds of people who never accept growing up. Regina was two years older than Naledi but she was not ready to accept that she was the big sister. It was even worse with David who's four years older than me, but he never saw that until he joined a gang. I just laughed as the two of them pulled my hand back and forth, fighting to get my attention. They were both wearing beautiful purple chiffon dresses and shoes to match them. They looked so cute and innocent, not yet brutalised by the world and its calamities.

'Congrats, my girl! I am so proud of you.' That was a surprise, Ma'am Masenya just got off the taxi. She gave me a handshake and the same lovely smile I saw three years back, when I graduated from high school. So this was well planned, I thought. I started to feel strange things in my belly, like a mixture of nervousness and excitement. I hugged her and thanked her for coming. She still looked very young. She had the kind of eyes that lit up the whole face when she smiled; bright big eyes with long natural eyebrows. Her skin as soft as silk, like a pear that's taken straight from the garden. She was the most beautiful teacher I knew, beautiful inside and out. What I saw next just made me cry my eyes out. I do not know whether there is any person in this planet that has ever experienced that kind of feeling before, the kind where fright and joy are mixed together. My brother just got off the taxi. That's when I realized that the whole thing was planned very well. These people got off the taxi like movie stars, one after the other. They just planned to give me a surprise of my life. I never imagined David here and no one ever mentioned that he was coming out of prison any time soon. There he was, my one and only brother, my mother's firstborn, the sign of my parents' strength, and he was smiling from ear to ear. He was so thin you could almost mistaken him for a skeleton. So many scratches on his face and the scariest of them all was right under the mouth. As if someone was trying to get rid of his chin with a butcher knife but happened to regain his humanity while he was halfway. After the longest hug I've ever had with anyone on earth, with a few drops of tears showering David's shirt, he said, 'Surely you will make a good Chartered Accountant, little sis. I am so proud of you. You are my heroin. You just changed my life and my vision too. Now I believe in success and in second chances. You have showed us that you can be what you want to be as long as you put your whole mind to it. I decided to go to university the next year and get my engineering degree. Thanks, little sis, you are a true inspiration.' I could not stop crying, such a stream of joy could also wear one out. I was more than happy that my life was touching so many lives, especially hopeless lives like David's. That gave a meaning to my life.

'Come on now, stop crying and come with me to the taxi otherwise you'll have one hell of a headache before you ascent to the stage.' David took my hand and walked with me to the taxi, and I got shocked when he opened the door. I did not know what to do. I did not know whether I should run or faint. I was so frightened, frightened in a way that my feet were shaking uncontrollably. I wiped the thin sweat that was on my face and rubbed my eyes to check if they were not deceiving me. The last man I expected to be here had come…my father. Yes, my father had come and he was nervously grinning at me. He looked much older and tired. The smile was a weary one too. He was thinner than his son and he could not stop shivering on such a hot sunny day. Alcohol had destroyed my father's life. The brown worn out jacket and the wrinkled black leather shoes made him look like one who had spent his entire life on the streets. It was more like the clothes were on a hanger, in a store on a liquidation sale. After a few minutes of observing him, the fear just vanished. I realized how tired and worn out my father was. He was powerless to even hurt a fly. I felt pity for him, and I wanted to cry but could not because I had run out of tears. For half of my life I have been crying; crying when my mother cried, crying when my mother died, crying after death and also when my brother got arrested, and those were just few tears from a stream. I've been hurt up to a point where I become rigid, more like a mountain rock which could not be easily moved. For my whole life I've been shedding tears of sadness and now my eyes just decided to spare only tears of joy. My heart was very painful though, I knew I used to think I hate my father and sometimes even wished bad things to happen to him. But to tell the truth I did not want to see him like this. I just realized that I loved my father more now than I hated him then. He was my father after all, nothing he had ever done could ever take away that love a child always has for a father. Nothing on earth was worth that, nothing.

'Hey, my beautiful daughter. It's me, your father. Come to me,' my father said with the same weak smile. 'Don't be scared, I won't bite you.' Of course, he wouldn't bite me without teeth. Some of his front teeth were out. Five years back he got involved in a fight with father Boxer, in a liquor store, and he knocked the teeth out with one fist. The man was given the name because he had huge scary fists, and it was said he could beat even Tyson. I don't know where my father got the guts to fight with such a man because everybody in the village feared him. Even at school his kids were treated like kings because of their father's "Goliath" reputation. It was said even their mother was like that. She died a mysterious death a few years back. The village gossipers said she was bewitched by one of father Boxer's concubines. It's said one day she found father Boxer red-handed and knocked all the concubine's teeth out.

'Hello, papa. I'm happy you came,' I said with a nervous smile. I did not know what the right words to say were. This was the man whom you would not just talk anyhow when you are with him. My mother knew that better. You do the right thing you get crucified, you do what seem more than right you go down. There was nothing good that you could ever do for my father, nothing seemed to impress him.

'My lovely daughter, you proved me wrong. You are very strong. Just like your mother, you never give up. Out of all my kids you were always the strongest, and when you were born we thought you won't make it. You were the smallest of all the pre-matured babies that were born on that day. You were always so sick and we thought you will die. Your mother cried day and night because the doctors assured her that you won't make it. We almost gave up on you but you pulled through. That is why we decided to call you Dikeledi (Tears) because you brought so much tears on us when you were little, which I now believe it's a wrong name for such a survivor like you. I know I am the last person you will expect to say this to you but I am so proud of you, my daughter and I mean it, from the bottom of my heart.' I just stood there like a rock without moving. I never expected to hear my own father talk about how proud he was of me. It was the first time I hear my father talking about my life as a baby, not even my mother would. She always avoided the subject of my life as a baby and now I know why. The memories were so painful for her to bear. Now I understood where my name came from. I always asked myself why they named me "Tears" but now I do. If you combine my name and surname they make a disaster, Dikeledi-Tears, Mafifi-Darkness, which means I am Tears Darkness. Learners at school used to mock me using my names and that really made me to hate being me with passion.

'My daughter, I know I had not been the best father you wanted me to be and I am very sorry for that. I was not there when you needed me. I abused you kids...' dad sighed deeply. 'How much I regret that now. I despised you and brought a woman at home just after your mother's burial, and the woman had left because now I'm sick. I wish you could forgive me for all the horrible things I have done to you. Forgive me for...' He choked and I could see it was hard for him. If it was possible he would turn back the hands of time. 'Forgive me for killing your mother. I know it's all my fault that she got hit by a car. Just forgive me, my children, please...' My father cried and it was for the first time I saw him cry. It was more than painful to hear him blaming himself for my mother's death. I knew I once believed that too. I once blamed him for mom's death but now I just realized everything happens for a reason. Mom died because it was her time to die, it was no one's fault. I just could not allow my father to keep on beating himself like that, he didn't deserve the torture, and no one did.

'Dad, it's okay. Please don't cry. You didn't kill mom. She died because it was her time. No one could have stopped it,' I said, wiping tears that were running down his wrinkled face. 'It's not okay, my daughter. I am a very wicked man and I deserve to die. I was so stubborn and abusive. I never believed in anyone of you. You see this brother of yours?' he said, pointing at David who was also crying. I was just confused; here were two big men in my life, crying like babies—the only two men in my life that I loved so much and respected for their guts. 'He could have gone to university but my typical mind towards education denied him a chance to shine. I used my past experiences to judge you kids. I never believed anyone in my generation could ever make it through university because no one ever went there before, not even your great grandmother. I am very sorry, my children. Please forgive me,' dad said, with a stream of tears running down his bony cheeks. I never thought I would see this day. I hugged him and said, 'It's okay, papa. We forgave you a long time ago. I love you so much and I did all this to show you that everything is possible. We forgive you.'

'Yes, dad, we love you and we forgive you,' David said,

hugging both of us. I was happy that this day was more than a graduation day; it was also a reconciliation day. That was what made it so special. It's amazing how the world behaves, one minute you are miserable, the next you are the happiest person alive. One minute you have no one next to you; the next minute you have the whole world besides you. Just look at all these people who came to my graduation, they were more than enough. What more could a girl want? All the people that I loved were there to support me and I could not stop thanking God for them. Did I just tell you Uncle Nick was there too? Yes, he came driving a blue van this time and I did not care whether he combed his beard or not; all I cared about was that he was also there to support his lovely niece. I just wish God could forgive people like Aunt Ruth who took delight in messing up people's lives. I could see my father was hurt by what she did to him. As much as I never liked her, I knew she made my father happy. Maybe my father brought her home so early because it was his way of mourning my mother. My father was more like David, they always avoided showing their emotions instead they would look for some sort of distraction to take their pains away. We all have our own way of handling situations and my father's solution of mom's death was bringing Aunt Ruth home as soon as possible to close the gap.

'Thank you, my children. I am so happy you forgave me. It really means a lot. Thank you.'

After all the drama, we all went inside the house and found the table well set. Everybody gathered around the table while the "brides" went into the room to prepare for the big day. But before that I recalled I needed to do something. I went and sat next Mama Regina at the table and said, 'Mama, I just want to take this opportunity to thank you. You know, since my mother died you have been there for us. You have been supporting me from the first day I entered through the gates of the university until this very day and you never complained. You've been a good mother to us for all these years, and truly I do not know of any woman with a heart as big as yours. Thank you for taking care of Naledi and thank you for everything you have done for us. May it not end with us. I love you, Mama.' Mama Regina could not say any word except shedding a few tears. They were tears of joy, tears of a proud mother who was happy that her part was successfully played. I wiped her tears with the tips of my fingers and went to join Sophie in the bedroom. We put our regalia on with pride, and guess who bought mine, my father. Mama Regina told me how my dad begged them to let him do this one good thing for his daughter. That really made me happy, beside the twenty rand note that my father gave me that time I matriculated, this was the greatest gift I've ever got from him. The graduations went more than we thought. My whole family and friends were there to support me. When it was my time to accent the stage, there was enough noise to block the ears. Mama Regina and Ma'am Masenya ululated, while Naledi and Regina screamed my name, David and Uncle Nick kept on whistling while Papa Regina could not stop smiling and my father could not stop crying. They were probably tears of regret and joy; he was realizing how much he could have cost me by denying me the opportunity to come to university, at the same time joyous that I went against his will. After the graduation, we went back to my roots, Molepo village, to celebrate my success. I had a wonderful graduation party, and almost everybody in the village was there, the invited and the intruders. Everyone was there to witness what to them seemed like a miracle. Some did not believe that "typical me" could come back from university with a degree. It was like a wedding day, the gifts that I got were so many that they would not fit in one room. All my high school teachers were invited and some of my former classmates were there. Mr Morema was there too and he bought me a laptop as a gift.

'Congratulations, Miss Mafifi! You are the most successful troublesome student that has ever made it in life since my teaching days. You broke the record, lady. Keep it up!' Mr Morema said with the widest smile I've ever seen on earth, it was more like one who was advertising the most selling toothpaste. I did not know what my former principal's definition for troublesome was, but I never thought I brought that much trouble during my school days except I lacked a proper school uniform. And I really don't know whether lacking a school uniform could be associated with trouble. Anyway, I was just thrilled with the laptop and I could not wait to work on it. He also invited me to come to school to give the learners a motivational speech. I was thrilled by that idea; I was always that kind of a person who liked sharing her success with others.

12

Everybody was gathered around the school assembly staring at me with curiosity. I smiled and moved a little bit forward so that I could start with my motivational speech, as the principal defined it, but to me it was not just a speech, it was rather a story of my life. More like a word of advice from an elderly sister to her little brothers and sisters. I smiled and said, 'I know you all know me. If you don't, just ask around they'll tell you. I probably have many names, of which some may no longer be relevant in these days.' Some of the learners giggled because they knew what I was talking about. When you are a nobody you will have certain names that suit the person you are by that time, and when you become a somebody you get new names that suit the person you are now. And everyone who dares use the "nobody" names when you are now a "somebody" will be chewed alive by the same people who gave you the names then. It's just funny the way life goes; the same people who were against you a few years ago are the one who are protecting you now.

'I attended the same school as you, same classes and same process. My school days were a horror. I did not enjoy waking up in the morning just because I did not have a school uniform. I did not choose not to have one, but no one would buy it for me. I envied other learners as they wore their ties and pullovers with pride. I envied them eating polonies and cheese at lunch breaks while I ate porridge mixed with water. Things got pretty bad when my dear mother died. I lost hope in life and felt like the entire universe was against me. I hated my own life but unlike many I decided to do something about it. You see, my own father told me I won't amount to anything but that did not stop me from pursuing my dreams. I chose to prove him wrong. I chose to succeed no matter what he said. Please, good people, don't get me wrong. I totally adore my father now even more than I hated him then. You know why? Because he is the reason I am successful today.' I saw other learners raise their eyebrows, probably asking themselves if I was hearing what I was saying.

'Yes, he is the reason for my success. You see, you must be grateful for all those people who ill-treat you because they push you to be the best you could be. But that depends on your attitude towards it, is either you choose to let their ill-treatment lift you up or pull you down. But please, if you choose to be pulled down, blame no one at the end but yourself. One wise man once told me that life is a choice. We are all responsible for our destiny. Every step that you take in life is a choice. I chose to pass Grade 12 and I also chose to go to university. I did not have money or support from my parents to take me there but my choice got me there. When I got there I still had to choose my friends. I chose to befriend my books rather than a bad company. I left nice times and went to library. I never had fancy clothes and delicious food to eat. Sometimes I slept with an empty stomach but that was never an excuse not to succeed. I did not have textbooks, so I borrowed and kept awake all night. I left boys and nice times because I knew where I was going. I saw people failing and giving up on their dreams. I also saw others die because they chose to live their lives recklessly.' I paused a bit and gave a moment of silence to my late friend Khensani, may her soul find peace.

'You see, beautiful people, with me there is always a day that is coming. I always have a specific day that I will wait for and I work very hard to make sure the day arrives as I planned. For vision bearers always have a certain day that comes in a specific time of their lives. The first day that I waited for in my life was the day I matriculated, the second day was the day I graduated from the university and now that the first and second day had arrived as planned, I am waiting for the third day which will be on the coming Monday when I start working, paving my route to chartered accountancy. The fourth day will be when I qualify as a Certified Chartered Accountant of South Africa. The fifth day will be after a few years when I establish my own company. And then there will the sixth, seventh day and so on until infinity. I am not stopping here, this is just the beginning. I am not there yet. Good people, you must never reach a stage in life where you are comfortable with yourself until you reach a certain stage that I call abundance. That's a stage where you lack nothing. One wise man once said people sometimes get satisfied with a drumstick not knowing there is a buffet waiting for them. For now my degree is just a drumstick and I will not rest until I get a buffet. One more thing, my good people, when you choose a career, choose something you love, something you enjoy. You see, I chose to do accounting because it is something I love, even my accounting teacher can confirm that, I love working with numbers and always did.'

'Oh, yes! That's my product, she loves playing with numbers,' Mr Mamabolo shouted from a line of teachers who were smiling from ear to ear. He was just a proud teacher, and who could blame him? I will also do that if I see one of my products finally selling on the market.

'Thank you, sir for the confirmation. You see, when you choose a career, choose something that you are passionate about. If your job is just a hobby to you, a paycheck will just be a bonus. Just imagine if you had to be paid for watching a movie…'

'That will be great!' one learner shouted from the assembly and others laughed.

'Yes, that will be great! Many people do a mistake of choosing a paycheck rather than what they love. Others chose their parents' dreams for a career and for the rest of their lives they are miserable. Every single morning they wake up going to a place they hate with passion and if they had a choice they will quit, but they couldn't because they are scared who will pay their bills. Their jobs become a burden for their entire lives. As for me, I will always look forward to every day at work because I chose to do a hobby for a job.' I noticed Mr Morema nodding his head. 'Lastly I will say, never let people determine your destiny, be responsible for your own future. Your life is yours and yours alone. It's not your parents', not your teachers', not your friends', not anyone's but yours and yours alone. You are the pilot of your own life, you decide whether your life lands safely or crushes on the way. I chose to be a vision bearer of my life and look where I am today. I am not bragging but trying to show you that you can be anything you want as long as you put your mind to it. Today I have a career; I'll be starting on Monday as a Junior Accountant at one of the top accounting firms in SA. I will be writing my CTA in months to come, and very soon I will be a Chartered Accountant. My fellow colleagues, choose to succeed no matter what. Choose to love because you too need to be loved, choose to give because you too need to receive and choose to forgive because you also need to be forgiven. Believe in yourself, have hope, have faith, trust in yourself and most all trust in God. Thanks to my teachers and all who believed in me. Thank you, papa. I love you and thank you for pushing me into success. Beautiful people, what I will leave you with is this: NEVER and I mean NEVER give up on your dreams. Believe in yourself because if you don't, no one will. Thank You.'